MW01516891

Waiting on the Other Side of Clarity

Broken Circles: Book 2

Vanessa M. Thibeault

Copyright © 2020 by Vanessa M. Thibeault
All rights reserved.

This book or any portion thereof may not be reproduced or used in any manner whatsoever without the express written permission of the publisher or author.

This is a work of fiction. Names, characters, businesses, places, events, locales, and incidents are either the products of the author's imagination or used in a fictitious manner. Any resemblance to actual persons, living or dead, or actual events is purely coincidental.

Printed in the United States of America
First Printing, 2020
Wooden Pants Publishing

ISBN: 978-0-9992039-6-5

DEDICATION

For those who showed me what it meant to be and those who showed me what it meant not to be. You know who you are.

WAITING ON THE OTHER SIDE OF CLARITY

ACKNOWLEDGMENTS

Thank you to Richard Keller for your work on this project, and a special thank you to Kristin for always being my "target audience."

CHAPTER 1

Music from the park drifted into Emily's ears as she moved the curtains aside and the warm summer evening called to her. But so did her children.

"Mom," Claire shouted in her sing-song voice. "Please come read us a story."

"I'm coming, sweetie." Emily peeked once more at the park's live music event, then closed the curtains. She left the doors open to hear more music.

Snuggling in her bed with Claire and Julia, she opened an illustrated version of *Alice in Wonderland* she purchased at a garage sale the day before. "Only one chapter, okay?" Emily conferred to her daughters.

"Aww!" The girls voiced.

"It's already eight, girls, and we promised to meet up with Susan tomorrow morning, remember?"

"Will Ben and Tay be there?" Julia asked.

"Yes. Andrea and Mackenzie, too." Emily brought the book closer and pointed to one of the pictures. A dressed-up rabbit with glasses made Claire laugh as she looked at it. "Let's start, or we're not going to have time to read even one chapter."

Julia and Claire snuggled in closer. Emily was full of expression and different voices for each character. Garnering their interest, she made sure to make even the most boring of stories interesting.

Gesturing elaborately as she finished reading, Emily got off the bed and held out her hands. Her eyes twinkled with impatience and amusement while the girls rolled around on the bed for a moment. Then they finally reached for her outstretched hands and hopped off. Together, they made their way across the hall to the girls' bedroom.

Bunkbeds lined one wall of the room while two small desks faced opposite them. Emily switched on a purple lava lamp on the dresser as they entered. The girls scrambled onto their beds.

"Sing to us, please?" Claire said as she snuggled down under her fleece blanket, eyes already heavy.

"Of course, honey," Emily said as she stroked Claire's blonde hair. The three songs she sang since the girls were babies calmed them. Soon, their eyelids were drooping. Emily kissed them both and left, leaving their door open just a touch.

Emily switched off the living room's overhead lights and allowed the area to be dimly lit by the fading day and the streetlamps outside. Flopping down on the couch, she ran her hands through her own blond locks and let out a sigh. She reached for a glass of merlot – forgotten when the girls called her. She took a long swallow of the rich liquid at the same time she stretched her legs out on the coffee table.

Emily closed her eyes and allowed her senses to reach out. She smelled the city below: people, vehicle exhaust, and lessening summer. Garlic and chicken wafted to her from the kitchen as the breeze blew through the open French doors. She could hear people outside enjoying the jazzy live music as the cars drove by. A siren in the distance brought her back to her apartment.

She took another long swallow of wine and grabbed her laptop from the end table. Emily placed it on her lap, opened her email, and started deleting the junk.

Her heart quickened at the site of a familiar email address. She ran her cursor over the hours-old message, finished her wine, and opened the email.

Emily,

I hope you've settled into your new place and the girls are doing well. Have you been to their new school yet? Have you met any other families? The kids here are good. I'm looking forward to when the twins start school this September so I can have a little extra time. I know it's been a while, and I'm sorry I haven't tried since you've been gone. I'm still struggling with it. Matisse and I were talking, and we thought all of us going on a trip together might be fun. It sounds like you and Conrad are amicable right now. Just a small trip, to the hot springs. The kids all seem to miss each other, and it would be great for us to catch up.

Love, Anika

Emily didn't have much time over the past few months to dwell on what might have been with Anika. Settling into their new apartment, registering the girls for school, and getting organized at her new job had taken all her efforts as of late. But she couldn't deny the strong emotion she felt when she saw Anika's name in her email.

Anika had opened so much in Emily, and then it was as though she had been a project no longer of interest and abandoned. Anika went back to an unsatisfactory marriage she had decided to make work, and Emily left to pursue another life, HER life, and to concentrate on raising her kids without the influence of their narcissistic father.

Emily hit the reply button:

Hey Anika,

It's great to hear from you! We are all settling in fine down here. The girls are getting excited to start school. I'm not sure about the family trip. Conrad and I seem to be OKAY(?), but I'm worried about giving him the wrong idea ... Can I think about it for a few days?

Chat Soon,

Em

Hot tears formed, and she closed her eyes while she thought of their whirlwind affair, Emily could almost smell the musky sweetness of Anika's perfume. The way her soft lips felt pressed against her warm ones as they became aroused together. Anika's small hands finding Emily's generous hips. Her moaning in pleasure as her hands found her most sensitive areas ...

Cheeks growing hot at the thought of Anika's light nipples in her mouth, Emily groaned out loud. Sitting up, she shook her head and placed it in her hands. She glanced at the computer screen again. It had only been a month since they had been together, but their relationship seemed so much further than that.

Emily closed the laptop and grabbed the bottle of wine from the kitchen counter. She retreated to her bedroom to satisfy the urges that never left her, though she had tried to leave them behind when she moved.

***

Walking the short distance to the park near their house, Emily lugged the backpack her and the girls' picnic lunch and a few toys.

"Wait for the Walk sign," Emily called to Claire who had reached the crosswalk about ten steps before her and Julia.

"Okay!" she replied, stopping to push the button on

the post. Running across the street as at the appropriate time, Emily shook her head and looked down at Julia who still held her hand. She reached the sidewalk and nodded ahead. Julia let go of Emily's hand to run ahead and meet the other kids already playing at the park.

Susan waved her free hand from the picnic table where she was setting up their meal. She tried to get the tablecloth to lie flat as she placed dishes on it. Emily laughed and held down one end. "Windy today!"

"It's Vancouver, there's always some kind of wind." Susan laughed and put a large plastic container of watermelon on the end Emily held.

They put out the rest of the food and opened their sparking juices. Emily sighed and watched the kids play.

"Hi, Emily," a child's voice said from behind her as its owner ran toward the other kids.

"Hi, and bye, Mackenzie," Emily called after her. She turned to see Andrea and another woman approaching.

"Hey!" Andrea said happily, embracing Emily and Susan as she set her bag down on the table. Andrea was a single mom. Mackenzie's father left when she was just a baby. "This is my sister, Izzy."

Izzy shook Susan's hand first, then Emily's. Once they connected, Emily's heart jumped a little as she met Izzy's eyes. Then she blushed at the realization she held onto Izzy's hand a touch longer than necessary.

Pulling away, Emily said, "Great to meet you. Are you from around here?"

Izzy ran a petite hand through her curly hair. "I live here. My editing job keeps me pretty busy, so I don't get out much."

"She's just anti-social and prefers her cats to people." Andrea gave her sister a playful shove and Izzy rolled her eyes. Turning to Emily she asked, "Are the girls ready to start at their new school?"

"They're super excited. I was worried they'd be nervous, but so far they can't wait to start."

"It's a great school with amazing teachers. I'm sure they'll have no problem making friends. Do you have any family around here?"

"No. I moved here for work. My sisters and brother are all in Calgary."

"Are you close with them?"

"Just in recent years, yes," Emily replied with a thoughtful look on her face.

"I'm lucky I have Izzy here with me." Susan put an arm around her sister.

Emily smiled then looked at her phone as a text message from Anika came in:

Hey Emily. I know you said you needed time to think over the family trip, but I saw a great deal for rooms at Harrison Hot Springs and wanted to book. Are you interested in going or not? I already spoke to Conrad, and he's really excited.

Emily sighed and made a frustrated face at her phone. She placed it on the table and looked toward the playground. The kids played well, swinging from the monkey bars in what looked like a kind of tag.

"Gentle hands," Emily called out as Julia pushed her sister. Julia waved and provided a quick "Sorry" before she could be tagged back by her sister. Emily shook her head and looked back down at her phone. A blinking light signifying another text message.

"Everything okay? Andrea asked.

"Yeah …" Emily paused to read the last message again. "My friend Anika, from where we used to live, texted to say she hoped I could do a two-family trip to Harrison Hot Springs in a few weeks."

"Two families? As in you, and the kids, and Conrad, and Anika's family?" Susan asked.

"Yeah. And I'm not so sure I want to dive into all of that with Conrad right now."

"Are you guys on good terms?" Andrea asked between mouthfuls of cracker and spinach dip.

"We seem to be. He hasn't brought up the move, and he's consistent with coming to see the girls. We seem to be fighting less."

"What about the girls? Do you think a trip like this would confuse them about you guys?" Susan chimed in.

"I don't know … I don't think so. I've been very upfront with them, and we won't share a bed or anything like that." Emily sighed and took a piece of celery, scooped up a large dollop of guacamole, and crunched loudly. She looked around at her new friends.

"I think there's probably little harm that can be done as long as you guys keep things plutonic.," Andrea replied. "I know you've said the girls miss their old friends and Anika, so why not give them a bit to look forward to and a reconnection with their old life?" Andrea looked at Emily sympathetically, "I know it will be hard."

"It shouldn't be all that difficult, as long as Conrad behaves himself. I have absolutely no intention to get back together with him." *It's my feelings for Anika that are going to get me in trouble,* Emily thought.

"Just make sure the romance of the springs doesn't get to you guys," Susan said with a raised eyebrow.

"Blah!" Emily replied with a disgusted look on her face that transformed into a smile. "Trust me! That's the last thing I ever want from him. Just the thought of anything sexual is enough to make me want to throw up."

"That's how I feel about my ex, too!" Andrea laughed as they toasted with their lemonades.

Emily swallowed the last of what was in her cup and snuck a glance of Izzy. In turn, Izzy watched her with sparkling amusement, her hands in her pockets. Smiling, Emily set her cup on the table and walked to gather the kids for lunch, deeply aware of the eyes that followed her.

CHAPTER 2

"Thanks for helping me get all the kids to bed," Emily said as Anika closed the door to their rooms and sat on the patio. She took a sip of her wine and tightly wrapped her sweater against the cool air of the early September evening.

"All good! It's been nice to spend some time with you again. I've missed you since you've been gone."

"I've missed you too, Anika." Emily reached for her. They entwined their hands and Emily gave Anika's fingers a small squeeze.

"What do you think about a weekend just to ourselves? I heard Conrad and Matisse talk about taking the kids on a final camping trip for the year during the first weekend of October. I thought maybe we could stay together. I'll tell Matisse that I want to do some early Christmas shopping."

Emily took a long sip of her wine and looked out over the view of the lake and mountains. She let silence sit between them for a few minutes before answering, "Are you sure that's what you want, Anika?"

"I've missed you, Emily," Anika replied without hesitation. "The need I have for you hasn't left me just because I wanted to work on my marriage."

"I'll tell Conrad and Matisse I have to work part of that weekend and you'll just be staying at my place by yourself," Emily replied quietly. She still felt the dull ache of yearning for Anika, but it wasn't as powerful as when she had left. It faded the longer she stayed away.

The space was good for her, she realized. Still, as Anika ran her fingers up Emily's arm and brushed the side her free breast over her thin t-shirt, Emily felt herself grow wet and aroused.

Anika stood, leaned over, and brushed her lips over Emily's. "The anticipation of you in my arms will be torture."

Emily moaned involuntarily and gave a sly smile as she ran her hands up Anika's inner thigh and gave it a little pinch. She laughed as Anika let out a small cry and jumped away. Sticking her tongue out, Emily leaned back on her chair and put her feet up on the railing.

"Do you need anything?" Anika asked.

"No thanks," Emily replied.

Moments later, Conrad and Matisse came through the door laughing and carrying takeout from the hotel's restaurant. "Thai chicken stir fry all around. And I grabbed four salads as well," Matisse explained.

"And cheesecake for dessert!" Conrad added

"Looks great," Anika smiled and gave Matisse a kiss. Emily looked out over the lake again. The light dimmed as clouds rolled over the mountains.

***

Conrad caressed her … fingertips down her thigh and up Emily's arm as she tried to ignore his advances. She'd had no intentions on sharing a bed with Conrad, but somehow it had happened.

He was slow and sly at first. He took the girls, sleeping on either side of Emily, out of the bed and placed them in the other. Emily woke to him crawling in beside her.

She didn't think anything of it. With a few drinks in her and being overtired from looking after the girls for so long with a demanding work schedule, all she wanted was a good night's sleep, not a dick in the back. She tried to pretend she was deep asleep, but her body betrayed her. It responded when she didn't want it.

She felt Conrad push against her. She tried to ignore him; But he started to pull Emily's pajama pants down and slip his hand up her shirt where he found her braless chest.

Just leave me alone. Emily thought, hoping he would know to not touch her anymore. But she felt helpless. She wanted to say something, but there would be a fight, and she didn't want a problem with her kids sleeping in the next bed.

I thought he clearly knew this wasn't what I wanted, she thought. It wasn't even his place to be starting this. She was trying to make the best of this situation and keep the two families together on a vacation. They all wanted to have fun, and it always seemed to be Emily who held everyone back.

"Stop," she whispered, still trying to ignore what he was doing. She felt her stomach lurch into her throat, like she was going to throw up. "No," she said more firmly as he pinched her nipple and pressed his naked penis between her legs. She wanted nothing less than to hit him and push him away.

"Stop," she whispered again, but weaker, as he pulled her pants further down and forced himself between her legs.

She knew his smell, his tells. She knew what he wanted, but she pretended to not know. To not want to know what was going on. She didn't want to be this person who gave him what he wanted, but here she was, not standing up for herself.

She didn't know what to do. Didn't have the strength to do what she should have done. There was no way she was going to be able to keep this amicable. Conrad was

11

going to try everything he could to keep her as suppressed and low as he could to feed his ego.

Emily let him finish and silently stood up. She pulled her pants up, went to the bathroom, and threw up. When there was nothing left, she dry-heaved until her stomach spasmed and her head throbbed.

She splashed cold water on her face and finished cleaning up. She shut the lights off and crawled into bed beside the girls, as far away from Conrad as she could get. She fell into a fitful sleep and woke to Julia hugging her tightly.

Rubbing the tired from her eyes, Emily rolled over and felt her body aching. Flashes from just hours ago came to mind, and she felt like she would be sick again. She lay flat on her back, willing the nausea to go away.

Claire kissed her and Julia recited every thought she'd had between being sent to bed last night and waking this morning. Emily smiled and held the girls close.

"Where's your dad?" Emily asked looking around the small room.

"He went to get coffee. He said not to wake you up. We didn't wake you up, did we?" Claire's voice held a hint of concern.

"No sweetie. You didn't wake me up. Let's get dressed, okay? Then we'll go find the others."

They got up and got dressed, Emily took care to change in the bathroom in case Conrad came in. She didn't want to provoke any more interest than he already had in her.

She dry-heaved once more. *At least he can't get me pregnant,* she thought as Conrad's vasectomy came to mind.

***

"Good morning, Anika!" Emily called cheerfully as she and the girls entered her friend's room. It bustled with activity from her three kids. Cartoons were running for entertainment, and Anika had coffee on. The rich scent made Emily's stomach churn with hunger. Reaching past Anika for a protein bar, Emily poured herself a cup of coffee and added a generous amount of Bailey's before sitting down. "How was your sleep?"

"It was pretty good, but Matisse kept harassing me for sex. He wanted to do it in the bathroom. I told him it was too small with the kids right on the other side of the door."

Emily made a face and laughed, "Very true, Anika." She took a tentative sip of her coffee. The liquid was strong, but smooth on her tongue, and it relaxed her as she sank into the bed, cross legged. "I think I'm going to head out a bit early with the girls."

"Oh?" Anika raised an eyebrow.

"I know we were supposed to get lunch together, but I just got an urgent email from work, and I have a few things I need to get done before this afternoon." Emily looked down at the comforter and didn't meet Anika's eyes. She felt dirty and embarrassed after Conrad, like she had let Anika down. Though really, the only person she had let down was herself.

"Emily … Are you okay?" Anika asked, her brow furrowed and eyes dark.

Before Emily could answer, Matisse and Conrad came in, laughing and carrying trays of coffee and muffins. Setting them down on the table beside the door, the kids crowded around like birds being fed breadcrumbs at the park.

Claire reached for a muffin and bumped an apple juice over. Matisse caught it, but not before some of it spilled out onto Conrad's shirt.

"Claire! Get out of there! Go sit down!" Conrad snapped at her, roughly snatching the muffin out of her hand.

Claire's face crumpled at his harshness, and she shrunk back from him. Though tears welled in her eyes, she stubbornly glared at her father, arms crossed over her chest. "No!" she said defiantly back.

"Go sit on the bed, or you're not getting a muffin."

"No!" she repeated.

Conrad moved toward Claire, and Emily jumped up from her spot on the far bed.

"Enough, Conrad." Emily pulled Claire behind her. She grabbed a muffin and a juice and took them to her daughter. "You can't talk like that," she said to her daughter. "You need to be careful and wait your turn."

Claire still glared but nodded as she ate her muffin. Emily ran a hand through her daughter's fine hair, then turned to make sure the other kids had what they needed.

Conrad stared at her, his eyes angry and mouth set into a hard line. Emily met his eyes with challenge and sat straighter on the bed. She drank her coffee and didn't take her eyes off him. He finally looked away at the request of Matisse as he handed out the coffees.

"What's in your coffee, Emily?" Conrad asked accusingly.

Emily hesitated. Something about the tone of his question made her feel uneasy. She didn't want to answer.

Before she had the chance to make something up or deflect the question, Anika came out of the bathroom. "Bailey's! Do you want some for your coffee, too?"

Emily gave Anika a look, and her friend shrugged her shoulders.

Conrad shook his head and ate his muffin. No one talked. The only sounds were those of eating. Emily finished and tried to excuse herself to pack.

She was only in her room a few moments when Conrad came in, his eyes just as intense as before.

"The girls and I are going to checkout out in the next half-hour or so," she said. "There's a good deal of driving to do. Plus, I have a few projects to complete before tomorrow."

"You're still going back?" Conrad asked. "After last night, I thought maybe you reconsidered breaking up our family."

Emily stared wide-eyed at Conrad and shook her head. Heat rose from her chest, up her neck, and flushed her face.

"Nothing about last night would ever make me reconsider leaving you. In fact, it has made my decision all that much more real and enlightening."

"You wanted it. Your body was slick and ready." Conrad smiled slyly. It was all Emily could do not to either throw up or throw something at him.

"It will NEVER happen again. You can't just compel me to want you. You don't get the power to force yourself on me ever again."

Conrad fumed while he watched Emily throw unfolded clothes, books, and toys into open suitcases. Checking under the beds for lost items, she stood and wheeled the suitcases toward the door.

Conrad stood in the way. "Excuse me," she said when she realized he wasn't going to move voluntarily.

He took a step closer. She stood taller and ready. Taking her hands off the suitcases, she readied herself to fend Conrad off.

He stopped with his face about six inches from hers. "You're my wife. You don't get to embarrass me and treat me like I don't matter. You can't keep the kids from me, either."

"I've never kept the kids from you. And I'm not the one treating you like you don't matter. You did that to me for years. Too many years. And, for the record, just because the piece of paper that says we're man and wife hasn't been destroyed yet, doesn't mean I'm YOUR wife. Grow the fuck up, Conrad. I'm not coming back to you."

With that, Emily pushed her way past him, brushing up against his body in the process. She felt his breath on her cheek, and he grabbed a handful of her hair. Emily stomped on his foot, and he let out a sharp cry.

"Don't you EVER touch me again."

"How much Bailey's did you have in your coffee this morning, Emily?"

Emily stopped in her tracks, turned, and looked him straight in the eyes "None of your fucking business."

She took the suitcases out to her SUV and let out a sob as she closed the trunk. Standing with her head against the vehicle, she allowed herself to cry for a few minutes. Then, with a deep breath, she calmed down. She looked inside the glovebox and found a pack of tissues to wipe her face.

Emily quickly made her way to her girls and hoped Conrad wasn't with them. She knocked Anika's door but didn't hear anyone. Confused, she knocked louder. There was no response.

Emily fumed as she returned to main floor. As she turned a corner, she saw all four kids in the pool along with Anika, and Matisse. She stormed through the door and started to gather her daughters' things.

"Claire. Julia, we have to get going." She sensed Anika watching her as she waited for the girls.

"What's up, Emily?" she asked, confused by the scene. "Conrad said you went to do some work stuff and would be back in a bit."

"I told you, Anika. I need to be home by this afternoon. Why would you believe Conrad?" Emily tried to hold her voice steady to keep her emotions from boiling over. She needed to seem calm and in control. It was the only way Conrad would be thrown off.

"I just thought maybe you changed your mind, that's all."

Emily felt hurt and betrayed. She knew there had to be some part that was Anika's fault, but she wanted to believe Conrad was the only bad guy in this situation.

"See you later, guys. Thanks for a great time."

Her eyes were filled with tears as she left. Anika and Matisse called their goodbyes, but neither of them apologized or offered to help.

CHAPTER 3

"Finally! Some time just for us!" Anika reached for Emily's hand as they strolled down the street.

Fall was in full swing and the October air was cool. Yet, the day's bright sunshine left the pavement radiating warmth. The balconies around them echoed the click of their heels and heightened Emily's senses. The feel of Anika's hand in hers spread warmth up to her cheeks.

Emily returned Anika's hand squeeze. Then, they released their hold at the same time. Emily's eyes lingered over Anika's white peasant top, the swell of her breasts just visible in the fading light.

"I'm glad we could spend the time together today while the guys have the kids," Emily said.

"Matisse never would have approved of us going out tonight even if they were back," said Anika.

"True."

Emily looked at the clear evening sky and noticed a flock of pigeons diving toward the trees in the park a few blocks up ahead.

"Who are we meeting again?" Anika asked, almost giddy.

"Susan, Viv and Andrea. I work with Susan and Viv, and Andrea is a mom friend I met at the park with the girls. They're all excited to meet you."

"I'm glad. I can't wait either," Anika paused to look at Emily. "Especially for later – it's been too long since I've been in your arms."

"Anika …" Emily's cheeks were hot with anticipation and need. It had been more than six months since the last time Emily had held Anika in her arms. Almost a year since she felt the soft caress of her lips --- of any one's lips, really – on her inner thighs, on her breasts. "Tonight will be one to remember." She craved to be made love to and longed to be held.

But these thoughts of longing nagged at her. She had made peace with her life, with how it was now. *Is it Anika I'm missing or just the connection we used to have? The physical connection with someone? What about how she was at the hot springs?*

Anika smiled while they walked a few more blocks to the pub where the other women had already secured a table.

***

"What do you think of finding a place where we might be more comfortable?" Emily suggested. Anika looked at her quizzically. "A place with women like us?"

"I'm not sure, Emily. Are you sure?"

"Sure. Why not?" Emily pulled out her phone and began to search for a same-sex bar.

"This will be interesting," Anika said.

Emily's heart pounded as she typed. Her eyes were blurry from drink and she swayed a little as she waited for the information.

"It's only a few blocks from here," Emily suggested. "Let's just walk."

Anika replied by taking Emily's hand and not letting go. It was late. No one would care, even if they came across someone they knew.

"It's called the *Backlot*," Emily informed Anika.

Anika gave her a raised eyebrow and quickened their pace as the online map showed they had reached their destination. There was a neon-lit door set back through a brick alleyway. A sign with an arrow and the word *Backlot* pointed down.

"This is a gay bar, ladies," the bouncer called over to them. He was bald and husky, but not intimidating, at least not to Emily and Anika. A hint of humor glinted in his eyes. They women were oblivious to what he meant, too concerned with the thought of being able to be themselves in a non-judgemental place.

"We know," Anika replied for both and they strutted their way in.

Men surrounded them. Pictures of Freddy Mercury, Elton John, and other famous entertainers, both straight and gay, filled the walls. Emily and Anika paid no attention, or rather, didn't notice the lack of women around them. They quickly found themselves at the bar.

"Two Corona and two shots of Jack," Emily requested loudly over the music's hum.

Two shots rapidly appeared, and Anika and Emily downed them just as fast. As Emily took the beers from the bartender, she dropped one through her fingers onto the floor. They soaked into her leather heels and stockings "Shit!"

The young bartender didn't miss a beat. He quickly placed another open Corona in front of her and handed a bar rag to a nearby bouncer.

Emily waved her apology and stepped out of the way. The bartender nodded and went to the other end of the bar.

The women found a table at the quieter end of establishment.

Anika giggled, "Emily?"

"Yeah?" Emily smiled as she took in the rest of the scene. The men dressed in everything from drag to cowboy hats.

Anika caught Emily's eye. "Umm, I think this might be a gay bar."

"Yeah." Emily and Anika burst out laughing and almost fell off their chairs. "Wait, though. Do you hear that?"

"What's that?" Anika asked raising an eyebrow

"No one's hitting on us. No one's talking to us. No one's trying to make small talk with us."

"I love it!" Anika laughed again. "As women, this is probably one of the safest places for us to be in the city."

"You're probably right." Emily finished her beer, and they sat in silence listening to the music. It wasn't the techno/pop they were used to at the regular clubs. The music had beat and meaning.

"Should we get going?" Anika asked a few moments later, seemingly reading Emily's mind.

"Yes." Emily reached over and squeezed Anika's hand. Their eyes held each others'. Memories of how they used to be flashed back to Emily and she blushed. "Let's get out of here."

Anika led the way out of the busy bar. No cat calls or rude comments followed them out. "Have a good night, ladies," the flamboyant bouncer said as they headed back to Emily's apartment.

They quickly walked together, yet every step seemed to take forever. Emily shivered with a combination of chilled air and the anticipation of warmth and desire to be home and in bed with Anika.

***

Emily unlocked the apartment door. Before it had a chance to close behind them, Anika had Emily pressed up against the entryway's wall. Searching hands and heavy kisses kept them there while shoes and stockings were removed, and skirts were hiked up to waists.

Emily let her head hang back, neck exposed, one leg up against the wall. Anika slowed and gently kissed Emily's neck, then pressed her head into her shoulder. Both allowed their breath to calm as their passion subsided for the moment.

Once their heartbeats eased, Emily led Anika to her bedroom and the en-suite bathroom's large tub. Starting the water and adding bubbles, she turned to Anika, whose hands were on Emily's hips. She took Anika's face in her hands and gently kissed her mouth and down her jaw.

Bringing her fingers to the front of Anika's blouse, Emily brought the hem of it up and over Anika's head. Her red hair fell around her breasts and over her shoulders. Emily discarded the shirt and undid Anika's bra in one swift motion.

"You haven't lost your touch," Anika laughed as she allowed her bra to fall off her arms to the floor.

"And you're still as beautiful as I remember you."

"You're the beautiful one, Emily. You always have been."

Anika brought Emily's mouth to hers and kissed deeply. Hot lips pressed together, Anika snuck her tongue between Emily's lips. It had been too long for since either of them had kissed or been kissed this passionately. Neither found what they offered each other since being together. The passion and need didn't leave them, no matter the distance or time. Absence had put fire in their desire for each other.

Emily's hands found Anika's ample bottom, and she ran fingertips over the curve of her ass, sending a shiver of goose bumps up the other woman. Anika grabbed Emily's shoulders with her fingertips to send a sharp twinge of sensual pain down her arms and back.

"Emily." A small moan escaped Anika's lips as she pulled her friend closer and buried her nose in Emily's blonde hair.

Anika pulled out Emily's ponytail and ran her hands through the fine soft locks. The wave from the braid caused the hair to bounce as Anika's hand massaged Emily's head.

Emily moaned in pleasure and dropped her head to Anika's chest. After a moment, her thoughts returned to the present, and she stopped the water.

She turned around so Anika could undo her zipper, Emily let her purple and black dress fall to the floor. She wore nothing but a purple lace G-string.

Emily stared at Anika mischievously, a smile slowly spreading over her face. Her blue eyes sparkled. She unzipped Anika's skirt and pulled it down, underwear and all. Her fingers skimmed down the front of Anika's belly and close to where Emily could see her partner had freshly shaved. Emily groaned in anticipation and stepped back.

Emily removed her G-string and sat in the bath. Opening her legs wide, she indicated for Anika to join her in that area. Once Anika sat down, Emily reached for the lavender body wash and poured a generous amount onto a pouf. Slowly starting on her back, Emily washed and massaged, bringing her hands and pouf to Anika's breasts.

Emily emptied her hands and ran her fingers slowly over Anika's nipples. They became hard and erect at the touch. Emily squeezed and rolled them gently between her thumb and forefingers. Anika leaned her head into Emily's shoulder to provide access to her neck and ears.

Nibbling slowly on her friend's lower neck and shoulder, Emily made her way up Anika's and placed gentle pressure with her tongue just under Anika's ear lobe as she continued to squeeze and roll her nipples.

Anika let out a moan of pleasure and pain and squirmed her hips backward into Emily. She responded to the pressure with her own hips and cupped Anika's breasts. Anika turned her head to kiss Emily, and fingers toyed with damp hair. Both women were covered in bubbles.

Anika got on her knees, turned, and found Emily's breasts with her own searching fingers. Cupping and enjoying their heaviness, she found Emily's mouth once more and kissed her deeply. Anika rolled Emily's nipples between her own fingers causing Emily to squirm.

"Let's get out," Emily whispered. She squeezed Anika's bum hard enough for her to cry out.

Two fluffy towels waited for the women as the cool air heightened their arousal. They dried themselves and discarded them on the floor in search of the warmth and comfort of Emily's bed.

Once beneath the light down comforter, Emily and Anika succumbed to their needs. Hands finding hands; legs finding legs; mouths finding mouths. There was no inch of either of their bodies that the other didn't kiss or touch.

Emily could feel herself nearing her climax as Anika licked at her wetness. The feel of Anika's tongue on her clit and the need in her body grew her to the brink of no return. Calling out Anika's name loudly as she came, Emily grabbed Anika's hair and held on.

Anika came to rest on Emily's chest. Emily's breathing slowed as she felt the comfort of Anika on her, damp red locks cooling her heated skin. Emily gently caressed Anika's shoulders and back.

Emily rolled on top of Anika and brought her mouth to her breast, then kissed her way down to her hips. She kissed down from Anika's inner thigh to her knee and back up the other leg. Running her fingers down the center and between her folds, Emily slipped two fingers effortlessly into Anika. She slowly pulled them out and back in. Anika moaned in pleasure as Emily rhythmically brought Anika closer to orgasm.

Leaving her fingers in, Emily brought her mouth to Anika's clit and sucked while flicking it with her tongue. Emily felt Anika tighten around her fingers. In return, she pushed moved them at a faster pace, holding onto Anika's clit gently with her teeth.

Emily felt Anika's spasm around her fingers as she cried out loudly, her voice deep and primal as Emily continued her pace. Finally slowing, her body now damp with perspiration,

Anika pulled Emily towards her. She wrapped her arms tightly around Emily's chest. Both their hearts slowed, and their breathing deepened as they drifted off.

***

Emily woke slowly the next morning, her comforter light, warm and soft on her naked body. From the open window she heard birds and the gentle drone of people starting their day. She also listened to Anika's deep breaths.

Emily could smell Anika and the remnants of their night. It was a mixture of lavender body wash, lingering perfume, and the heady aroma of sex.

Emily rolled over and put her arms around Anika. She took in the scent of her thick hair spread over the pillow and kissed Anika's shoulder. The soft skin under her lips aroused Emily once again, and the throbbing between her legs reminded her of the previous night's activities. Emily hugged Anika and rested her cheek on her partner's back.

Anika stirred, entwining her fingers with Emily's and pushed closer into her. "Good morning, beautiful," she mumbled sleepily through half closed lips and shut eyelids.

"Good morning," Emily replied, kissing Anika's back and leaving a trail over her shoulders. Grasping Anika's breast with her entwined hand, Emily found her nipple and rolled it gently. It caused a groggy moan to escape Anika's lips.

"Trying for a repeat?" Anika giggled and rolled onto her back, eyes still closed.

"Always," Emily replied happily.

"What time is it?" Anika asked as she ran her fingers over Emily's hip and down her leg then back up again.

"Too early and too late all at the same time." Emily sat up to check the time. "Matisse and Conrad should be back in a couple of hours."

She flopped back down, and Anika snuggled in closer to her. Emily wrapped her arms around her friend and closed her eyes to the world around them for a few more minutes. *I thought I had forgotten. I thought I was fine with her gone,* Emily thought to herself. *Men have never made me feel like this.*

Emily felt goose bumps rise on her body as Anika ran her fingers over her bare chest and down her belly. Opening her legs, Emily allowed Anika to enter her easily. Thoughts of the times they had been together in the past flooded Emily and she quickly allowed her release to come.

Emily and Anika rolled over together, and Emily kissed her way down Anika's stomach, Emily reached her soft, wet folds and dived in, lapping up the goodness of their arousal. Anika began to squirm beneath Emily's mouth, her hips raising and thighs closing at the pleasure. Finally, in a loud burst of finality, Anika let go and found her release.

***

As she got dressed, Emily stole a quick glance at Anika. She stirred such emotion in Emily, it was difficult to fathom that their lives weren't as intertwined any longer.

Being with Anika had awakened Emily to a reality that something was missing in her life. Anika was part of it, but she wasn't an option. Anika had decided that Matisse and her life back home was where she needed to be. Emily had been weak and needing to allow her to spend the weekend. The result was they fell back into what came so naturally with each other.

Emily knew Anika was a dead-end road for her and, although it saddened and hurt her to think she may have wasted some of her time, she was also thankful of the lessons it taught her: patience, desire and the reality that something was missing while married to Conrad.

She wasn't the same person she was at the beginning of her marriage. Nor was she the same person as she was at the start of her relationship with Anika. She was a new person. Someone who looked for herself once again. Someone searching for something she didn't realize was missing.

***

Emily fell into her usual nurturing ways in the kitchen. Eggs, bacon, avocado and tomatoes found their way onto plates. Emily slid over-easy eggs out of the pan as Anika walked from the bathroom into the kitchen. Her freshly washed face and tied back hair left no hint of the night before, but Emily could see the glow and sparkle when their eyes met; need and desire still smoldered in Anika's eyes.

Emily smiled. "Well! Good morning there, sexy. Coffee?"

"Yes." Anika wrapped her arms around Emily's waist. Emily closed her eyes and leaned her head back into Anika. She felt lips and hot breath on her neck. The old familiar stirring brought back mixed memories.

"Anika," Emily whispered, not wanting to disturb the moment but having already brought herself out of the ecstasy and dream of last night. "Our breakfast is getting cold."

Emily felt Anika tense and hold her breath for a moment. Abruptly stepping away, Anika turned and walked silently to the bar.

"Anika. I just … I'm sorry. Please don't pull away from me after last night."

"You've been different these last few days. Really different since the hot springs," Anika said. Emily sat in silence, playing with her coffee cup, not making eye contact. "We didn't have to do this weekend if you didn't want to, you know," Anika continued with indignation.

"Things have been different since I moved," Emily said. "You've been working on your marriage and continuing with your career change, and my job has been busy. We always said there might come a time when we start to drift away. I'm not saying that's what's happening now …"

Emily put her hands up in defense to shoo away the notion, though it was what she felt.

"I think that … there were some things that happened with Conrad and I at the hot springs, and I've been feeling uneasy about it. I won't be going on any more family trips with your family if Conrad is involved. It's too hard and too confusing for the girls." *And Conrad won't leave me alone,* she added to herself.

"Things are going to change between us," Anika said. "We knew that all along. You just seem distant from me. I'm still your friend, and you can tell me anything you need."

"Thank you." Emily hugged Anika "Now eat up before it gets cold," Emily joked as she poked a piece of avocado from Anika's plate and teasingly popped it into her mouth.

CHAPTER 4

"If we decide to go this route," Emily paused and pointed to the smart board where the editing chart was laid out, "then I think we have a better chance of securing current contracts and using it as a magnet to pull other clients in."

The room nodded as she closed her file and they murmured agreement of her proposal. Jay, Emily's boss, got up and shook her hand, "Thank you for this. We hadn't even considered it as a possibility to retain clients and build our brand. I'll let you know what our decision is by end of today. Can you be in contact with the office tomorrow morning?"

Emily looked down as her phone vibrated for the fifth time in the last hour. "Yes. Of course. I'll pop in first thing tomorrow morning. Thank you."

Emily packed up her things. As the last person left, Emily checked her phone and discovered four missed calls, three voicemails, and two text messages. They came from the school, Anika, and Andrea.

Emily listened to the first message and cringed.

"Hi Emily. This is Principal Hawes. Julia and Claire's dad picked the kids up today early from school. We didn't have any previous indication this was going to happen, but since you're the primary parent, we thought you should know. We also called your emergency contacts, Anika and Andrea. Let us know if there is a problem."

"Fuck!" Emily cursed under her breath as she switched to the next message and heard Anika come on the line.

"Hey Emily. Your daughter's school called me. I guess Conrad decided to pick the girls up. I assume you're in a meeting. Give me a call if you need anything."

Emily felt tears build as she listened to Anika's nonchalant response when it came to the girls.

Why would she think this wouldn't be serious? Emily angrily wiped the tears away and aggressively tapped the phone screen for the next message. It was from Andrea.

"Emily. You're not going to be happy about this, but Conrad picked the kids up. I'm making a few calls and trying to figure out where he took them. Let me know what I can do and call me as soon as you can."

Emily slammed her hand down on the table and stomped her foot in frustration just as a co-worker, peeked her head into the room. "Everything okay, Emily?" she asked.

Emily shook her head, "Some issues with my ex and the kids … I have to leave for the rest of the day. Email me anything I need for the clients and the rest of the prep for tonight, and I will answer anything that might be urgent before I go to bed."

"Sure. I'll have everything off in the next hour. Don't forget to send the notes from today to Jay."

"Thanks for the reminder. I'll get it done."

Her co-worker nodded and stepped out, then came back in for a moment, "Let me know if you need anything. I've been through a messy divorce with my kids and I know how hard it can be."

"Thank you," Emily said quietly and nodded. She packed up the rest of her things and called Conrad as she entered the elevator. It went straight to voicemail.

"Shit," she mumbled as she waited for his message to play. "Hey, Conrad. The school called, as well as the girls' emergency contacts. You picked them up early? Just wondering what's going on. You didn't discuss picking the kids up with me. I'm a little worried. Call me back."

Emily hung up and impatiently jammed the button for the main floor again. She texted Andrea and then Anika with the hope one of them had been in contact with Conrad.

Let me know if you hear anything ...

Emily tossed her bag in the back of car and started the engine. Sitting for a moment, she thought about all the places he may have taken the girls. *It's a Thursday, so he wouldn't have left town with them. Where had they said they wanted to go?* Emily thought to herself as she backed out of the parking spot.

Leaving the parking garage, she mentally ran through a list of all the places the girls loved visiting with their dad. Hitting the steering wheel, she braked hard as the car in front of her stopped at a red light.

"The aquarium," she said out loud, remembering they had just put in a new jellyfish display that both the girls wanted to see. Emily told them she was too busy the last few weeks and remembered overhearing them tell their dad on the phone how much they wanted to see it. She walked away, trying to be respectful and to give the girls time with him.

Thinking back, the girls did act a little funny and secretive this morning.

Emily kept checking her phone as she drove the twenty minutes to the aquarium. Cruising around the parking lot, she spotted Conrad's truck. Parking as near it as she could, she texted Andrea and Anika to let them know where she was, then she took pictures of his truck before heading into the aquarium in search of her daughters.

Entering quickly, she explained the situation to one of the cashiers. Asking if they had seen them enter, the young man at the next kiosk remembered them.

"I took his payment about forty-five minutes ago. The girls were super cute and excited about the seals."

"Can you page him here?" Emily asked, trying to keep as calm as she could.

"Yeah, we can do that," the woman said as she picked up the phone and sent a message over the building's PA system. "If you want to go look for them, I'll call security and make sure no one leaves until we find them."

"Thank you," Emily called out as she rushed off in the direction of the jellyfish exhibit. As she looked around at the small group of people, she caught a glance of a little blonde head ducking behind a pillar down the hall from where she walked,

"Julia?" Emily called out as she quickened her pace. Excusing herself through a group of tourists, Emily caught another glance of the blonde head, closer now. She broke into a run.

"Julia?" she asked as she grabbed the girl's arm.

"Mommy!" Julia cried out, wrapping her arms around her mother's neck as she bent down to take her daughter into her arms.

"Where's Claire?" Emily asked.

"Over there. Come on, Mom. Come see this," Julia put her hand in Emily's and pulled her in the direction of Claire.

"Hi, Mom," Claire said with a big smile as she reached her hand in to touch the sea anemone, "Dad picked us up from school, and all the kids in my class were soo jealous of me getting to leave early."

Emily wrapped her arms around Claire and kissed her head, "That's pretty neat, Claire. Where is your dad?"

Claire looked in the direction of the washrooms, "He had to use the bathroom. He told us to stay here and wait."

Emily followed Claire's eyes and watched Conrad come out of the bathroom. He met her eyes and briefly hesitated before strutting over to Emily and the girls.

"What the hell are you doing, Conrad?"

"Taking the girls to the aquarium. Seems pretty obvious, don't it?" He put his hands in the pocket of his hoodie and shrugged his shoulders.

"You didn't think it was important to tell me, their mother, you were taking them from school?" Emily crossed her arms across her chest and stood straighter. She struggled to keep her voice from shaking, "You didn't think that it might be alarming for their emergency contacts when the school called them as well?"

"I'm their dad, Emily. I have the right to see my kids whenever I want."

"Within reason, Conrad!" Emily half yelled. Then, lowering her voice as a few of the other aquarium-goers looked on, she continued, "You can't just take the kids out of school on a Thursday without telling me. What if they had appointments? What if I had made other after-school arrangements for them?"

"You need to let it go. They're my kids, and I don't have to okay anything with you. It's not MY choice they're living with you."

"We're not talking about this here. You know damn well why the girls are living with me, and you certainly didn't have much to say when it was convenient for you," Emily spoke hushed, yet her stomach churned as anger threatened to get the best of her. "I'm taking the girls home. I don't want to have to take you to court, Conrad. That doesn't benefit anyone." *Except for me,* Emily thought bitterly.

"Doesn't really seem fair to the girls to take them home when they're already here, does it?" Conrad replied smugly as he placed a hand on Claire's shoulder and made sure she was listening.

"Aww, Mom! I don't want to go!" Claire crossed her arms over her chest and pouted, her eyebrows furled deeply.

"We can come back on the weekend, okay? We already had things we needed to do this afternoon. Remember what we had planned for dinner in the crockpot? And what about your homework?"

"I don't care!" Claire exclaimed angrily.

"I don't want to go either, Mom," Julia whined, pressing her body closer to Emily.

"I'm sorry, girls, but this isn't a choice. It's time to go. You can say goodbye to your dad in the parking lot." Emily walked away, both girls in hand. Claire glowered and resisted until Emily let go of her wrist and she sulkily followed her mother.

Conrad hung behind, and Claire slipped her hand into her dad's. Emily looked back to see Claire just sticking her tongue out behind her back and Conrad laughing about it.

Pick my battles, Emily thought as she supressed the urge to address the disrespect here and now.

She paused at the front desk to let them know she had found her children and thanked them for their pages and effort. The man and woman Emily had spoke with earlier eyed Conrad as he passed by, Conrad paid no attention to them.

In the parking lot, Emily quickly moved the girls along to her vehicle. "Say bye to your dad, girls," Emily coaxed reluctantly, crossing her arms over her chest, secretly hoping they wouldn't want to.

"See you soon, girls," Conrad called as Claire and Julia climbed into Emily's car. The girls waved and turned to put their seatbelts on.

"Don't you EVER fucking do that again!" Emily said between gritted teeth.

"Grow up, Emily. You can't tell me what to do."

"You have to start thinking about what is best for the girls. Taking them out and not telling anyone … What if something happened? No one would know. And you weren't answering your phone and didn't tell anyone what was going on."

"Don't worry. The decision making won't just be up to you for much longer."

"What the fuck is that supposed to mean, Conrad?" Emily stood back watching her ex-husband. He had a smug look on his face. She'd seen it before: he felt confident he knew something more than her right now. He thought he was one up on her.

"You know what? Fuck you, Conrad." Emily got into her car. She pulled out of the parking lot and headed home.

The girls chatted happily in the backseat, talking about what they had seen at the aquarium today and what they were hoping to see when they went back on the weekend. Emily listened to them and was once again amazed by how quickly their moods could turn. Something so big seemed to have little effect on their outlook on life. They were still going to the aquarium and that was all that mattered to them.

Entering their apartment, Emily decided she needed to have a stricter talk with the girls about leaving the school with anyone. "Girls?" she called as they took their bags to their room. "We need to have a little chat."

"What's up Mom?" Claire asked as she flopped herself down on the couch next to Emily.

Julia sat down on the other side of Emily and snuggled in as she started, "I know it was your dad who picked you up at school today, and I know it seems like that should be okay. But …" Emily paused, "I need you guys to make sure you never leave with anyone unless we've discussed it in the morning or you get a note from the office from me, okay?"

"Why?" Julia asked

"Well … It's important I always know where you are, so I know you're safe. If someone comes to the school to pick you up and I don't know, then I would worry. Some people aren't safe and, although you do have safe people in your life who might want to pick you up, I need to know where you are. Okay?"

"What if dad comes to pick us up again?" Claire asked. "I liked seeing dad today. He was fun."

"I know this probably seems a little confusing, and I know you love your dad, and he loves you, but it's all about keeping you safe. If your dad comes to the school to pick you up again, you need to stay with your teacher or go to the office. Then they will call me, and we can discuss what we need to do. Does that make sense?"

"Yeah," Claire said, leaning back and bringing her book up blocking Emily's view of her face.

Emily sighed and sat back with Julia snuggled up next to her. *I hope they understand,* she thought to herself. "You guys getting hungry?" she asked aloud.

"Yeah!" Julia cried hugging her mom and jumping up.

CHAPTER 5

Emily scarfed the blueberry pastry down on her way to meet her daughters' principal. Looking in the rear-view mirror to make sure she didn't wear any of it, Emily headed into the school.

She paused at the front desk to check in. "I'm here to see Mr. Hawes please."

"I will let him know you're here, Mrs. ..."

"Ms. Eckhart."

The administrative assistant smiled and picked up her phone. Emily sat and looked around. Students quickly made their way up and down the hallways to their classrooms. It was the organized chaos of an elementary school in the morning. Emily shook her head and smiled, remembering her own days in elementary school.

"Ms. Eckhart?" Mr. Hawes interrupted Emily from her memories.

"Yes." Emily stood and offered a half-hearted smile as she followed the principal into his office. He waved her to a chair and sat behind his desk.

"What can I do for you?"

"Last week, the girls' father showed up and took them out of school early without my permission. I want to know how that could have happened, why it took so long for them to notify me and how to prevent this from happening again."

"Do you have your husband –"

"Ex-husband."

"My apologies. Do you have your *ex-husband* down as an emergency contact or an authorized pick up person?"

"I don't think so, no. He's listed as their father and an emergency contact for anything major. I didn't specify if there were any restrictions, but I didn't think he was authorized to take them without my permission." Emily played with her hands in her lap and willed away the buildup of tears as she remembered last week's panic.

"Oversights can occur if we aren't aware of the family dynamic. Especially if the children don't act out of the ordinary when they're picked up."

"I understand that, but I'm incredibly disappointed and was distressed that I had to track them down with their father. I want to work together to make sure this doesn't happen again," Emily caught a tear sliding down her cheek with a tissue.

"Should I note in their records that you must be notified if they're picked up by their father?"

"No. it needs to say that no one, other than myself, can remove Julia and Claire from the school. If I need someone to pick them up other than myself, I'll call."

"Do you have a court order of any sort that we can add to the file?"

"No ..." Emily's stomach turned as she worried it might be an issue. "I don't want to get the police or court involved if I don't have to, but I need to know my girls are safe.

"Of course." Mr. Hawes replied. "But unless there are safety issues and court orders in place, we can't restrict access. You currently have an Anika listed as an emergency contact. Is that still relevant?"

"Yes …" Emily paused and thought back to Anika's odd behaviour. "I need to add a second emergency contact that lives closer. Make Andrea Merton the primary and Anika the secondary."

Emily provided the information, and Mr. Hawes updated the computer records. After she signed papers authorizing the change, Emily thanked the principal and left.

Out in the fresh air, she breathed a deep sigh of relief. She knew the school would do their best to keep Claire and Julia safe while in their care. It still worried her that Conrad might try to get through, but it reassured her that there were steps in place to make it more difficult for him.

***

Emily's phone rang a few hours later while working at her kitchen table

"Ms. Eckhart?" the woman's voice asked after Emily answered.

"Yes?"

"My name is Sylvie Luden, and I'm with the Ministry of Family and Chid Services. We received a call about a recent school incident with your daughters and their father."

"I didn't ask the school to call." Emily's face reddened and she stood to pace. *I didn't want anyone involved.* "It was mostly miscommunication between their father and me." Emily was curt, her voice tight.

"Mrs. Eckhart …," Sylvie paused, and Emily could hear typing on the other end of the phone. "Emily, I know separations and divorces can be difficult, and I'm not here to take your children or deal with custody. My only concern is for the girls' ultimate safety. That means making sure they're secure at school and in the care of their guardians."

"I understand that. There's just been some ...," Emily searched for words to describe the relationship between her and Conrad. "... a bit of a communication breakdown."

"That's quite common during separations. You're not alone. It tends to be especially difficult when the woman decides to leave. Do you feel your ex-husband might try to take the girls from the school again?"

Emily hesitated. She had always tried to deal with things on her own, especially when it came to Conrad. She knew the damage the social services system could do to families. She also knew the help they could offer.

I'm a good mother. There's no reason to take the kids

She rolled a pen back-and-forth between her fingers and shifted from one foot to the other. "I think it is entirely possible. That's why I went to the school."

"Do you have any court orders in place for custody? Any visitation laid out?"

"No. I thought ... I didn't think we needed it. What I offered seemed fair, all things considered. He never argued with me. I didn't think it would be a big deal."

"That's alright. It's always better if you can resolve those issues outside of the courts, but there are times, especially when one partner might not be the most cooperative, that it comes in handy."

"I appreciate that, but I'm still not really interested in heading to court." Emily paced the length of the living room, stopping to absentmindedly dust off a bookcase shelf.

"My call is mostly to make you aware that the school contacted us with concerns and to offer support and resources if needed."

"Thank you. I'm not really sure what I need right now. I hope Conrad sticks to our agreed plan and checks with me the next time he wants to take the girls."

"If he shows up at the again, they'll contact me as well as you at the time. My advice to you would be to get your verbal agreement down on paper and have him sign it. Kind of like an added piece of insurance. Verbal agreements rarely hold up if you have to go to court."

"That's a great idea, thank you."

"If you have any questions, concerns, or feel like you would like more information added to your file regarding Mr. Eckhart, feel free to give me a call."

"I'll keep that in mind." Emily took Sylvie's phone number and email address and hung up. Going out onto the deck, the cold November air hit her. She shivered as she leaned over the railing and looked down. Thoughts of Conrad and the girls clouded her mind.

Why am I still protecting him? she asked herself.

CHAPTER 6

Emily rolled her bags to the door and kissed Claire and Julia. "You girls behave for Anika, okay? She's been looking forward to this for a long time." Claire and Julia hugged their mother and voiced their I love yous.

"Don't worry, Em," Anika reassured her, "We will have a great time!"

"I really appreciate you taking the time to be here with them. I'll only be gone four days," Emily replied.

"It worked out great with the classes I needed to attend."

"Do you have all the numbers I left for you?" Emily asked.

"Yes. The afterschool program gets out at five, right?"

"Yep. I wrote everything down in the notebook by the fridge. If you're really stuck, Andrea's phone number is in there as well. She's still in town today and tomorrow, so if you need anything –"

"Things will be fine," Anika cut her off, talking briskly at the mention of Emily's new friend.

Emily gave Anika a curious look, then shrugged it off. Her friend and lover – though she wasn't sure how much she was of either right now – hadn't been her first choice for the girls, but she ended up being her only one since Andrea was headed out of town with her daughter, Mackenzie. In addition, Conrad didn't, or rather, refused to take time off work to help. She was appreciative that Anika made her schedule work to look after the girls, especially since she was willing to be at Emily's.

It had been a long time since she left the girls with anyone for an extended period, and Emily nervously played with Julia's curls as she talked. Julia hugged her leg and Claire held her arm.

At least I know Conrad is working and won't be around, she thought as Anika rambled on about what she and the girls had planned to do. Emily felt unsure whether Anika would respect her wishes if Conrad did decide to show up, but at least she wouldn't have to worry about that.

"What about you? Are you looking forward to the time away? You probably won't be sleeping in, but at least it'll be uninterrupted, and meals are cooked for you."

"It will probably be too quiet," Emily laughed and gave each of the girls one more squeeze. Reaching for Anika, Emily hugged her friend, "Thank you."

Anika smiled as they broke apart and she kissed Emily's cheek. "Have fun and try to relax."

Emily laughed again as she moved through the door that Anika held open for her. She waved with her free hand turned toward the elevator.

***

Emily uncapped the eyeliner and gently pressed it to her closed lid.

"Shit," she muttered and reached for a cotton swab, rubbing it in the lotion open on the counter. She steadied her hand and finished then took a step back and looked at herself in the mirror approvingly.

Enhanced by the make-up, her blue eyes shimmered and cheekbones that made most women jealous, were highlighted. Only the dark circles under her eyes (mostly hidden by the cosmetic counter) and the start of crows' feet and laugh lines gave away her age.

Emily made her way to the tiny counter that served as her bar and kitchen for the week and poured another generous portion of whiskey into her glass. Skipping the ice this time, she didn't bother to recap the bottle. She turned the music up and danced herself to the bed where her clothes were. Conservative and edgy, it showed just enough curves shown to intrigue.

Pausing with her pants part way up, the vibrating of her phone interrupted her, and she nearly fell over as she tried to go for it on the dresser. "Hello?"

"Hi, Emily?"

"Yes, speaking."

"We're meeting down in the lobby for dinner, are you ready to go?"

"I'll be right down! Thank you!" Emily responded

"Sounds good," answered the voice on the other end.

Emily tried to calm herself. She hadn't been sure if someone would call. She hoped, and been halfway invited, in a casual 'I'm not sure what you're doing, but there's a few of us going for dinner' sort of way. However, doubt played in the back of her mind.

She pulled her Louis Vuitton heels on and checked her hair one more time in the mirror. Giving herself a big smile, she left the room and walked down the hall.

***

"Hi!" Emily sat down on an over-stuffed lobby chair and looked around for a server from the bar area. "Everyone looks refreshed. How was the rest of the day?"

The conference had been a busy whirlwind from classes about team building and morale to cold-calling and customer relations.

With only a short break between meetings tonight and tomorrow morning, everyone looked forward to relaxing and unwinding.

"It's been a long couple of days. This glass of wine has certainly been earned!" Lindsay, one of her co-workers, took a long sip. Her heavy body shook as she laughed off the stress from the week.

"How about you, Emily? Are you getting much out of the courses so far?" Jay asked, a sleeve of ale in his hand.

"I'm learning a lot! I feel like my brain is almost too full to absorb anything else. I'm glad we have a bit of a break before tomorrow's debrief and Friday's information drop." Emily spotted a server and waved him down to order a glass of red wine.

"I agree. It's been great that all of us have gotten the opportunity to grow as a team. I like that we've had the chance to get everyone from the office on a level playing field. Management and the front line, learning together."

"I'd like to make it through the notes I've taken. I feel like I'm not going to be able to make any sense of them," Lindsay chimed in.

Emily nodded and looked around while Jay and Lindsay made small talk about the conference. As her scan widened, she monitored the elevator for Blake. He was the one who mentioned the dinner plans to her.

"Do you agree, Emily?"

"Sorry?" she replied when Lindsay's voice returned her to the present. "I didn't catch all of that."

"The last presentation today, by Blake. I was telling Jay that I thought it had the most to offer with the examples given and research suggestions he gave us to take home."

"The importance of team building and being connected will be priceless," Jay confirmed.

"Yeah," Emily replied, still distracted, "I certainly took the most notes from his class. I didn't have the capacity to go back through everything, though."

She uncrossed and crossed her legs again, careful to

keep her wineglass steady, and repositioned her skirt. When she looked up, she saw Blake walk off the elevator, phone in hand. His short sleeve shirt was buttoned to the top, the beige slacks hung off his hips and met his Vans at just the right place. Calm and collected, he scanned the lobby seeking his group out. Smiling and giving a slight raise of his hand in a gesture of greeting, he excused himself through the people in his way.

Once again, Blake avoided eye contact with Emily, and it drove her nuts. Although she knew he was obviously attracted to her, he played it cool and kept his distance. It was a perfect, just enough, sort of distance. Frustrating for her, as she didn't want to come across as desperate or too interested, especially with her other colleagues here. And being honest with herself, she really didn't know what she wanted.

Was her attraction to Blake simply the idea of who and what he represented? Was it even really a sexual attraction, or was this the only way Emily could express attraction? Through sex? Sighing, she crossed her legs the other way and positioned her body in the opposite direction from Blake.

"Can we have a table?" Blake smiled as he spoke to the server. He raised an eyebrow to Jay as he made his request, and Jay nodded in agreement, picking up his beer and standing.

***

"You know, there aren't any confirmed cases of marijuana actually being laced with fentanyl. That was another one of those plays by the media and society's mob mentality to blow things out of proportion," Jay stated.

Blake leaned back on his chair with one arm over the back. They'd all had more than a few drinks and he was more relaxed now than Emily had seen him all week. Emily noticed he had undone his top button, and she watched him swallow the last of his merlot. He toyed with the glass i for a moment as what he said sunk in with the other three.

"That's fair. Yet, although, there's been no confirmed cases, don't you think it's something to be looked at?" Emily asked. She took a sip of her wine. Suddenly aware of how tipsy she was, she carefully placed her glass back on the table. "It could be that there hasn't been enough evidence to confirm any of that. Rumors always stem from some sort of truth, don't they?"

"Facts are facts, and if there isn't any concrete evidence, then there's no case and no reason for anyone to believe the rumor," Blake countered impatiently. He set his glass back on the table a little harder than necessary.

Emily took another long sip of wine, picked up her last tempura prawn and ate it slowly. She tried to make eye contact with Blake, but he was back to ignoring her. Instead, he turned to Jay and started a conversation about the night's hockey game.

Emily shook her head, embarrassed, and finished her wine. She had once again been dismissed by this man, and she had no idea why it bothered her so much.

"So, Emily," Lindsay started, "who has your kids during the conference?"

Emily cleared her throat and wiped the corners of her mouth with her napkin. "I have a close girl friend with kids around the same age from where we once lived. She agreed to come and watch them. I had to miss the first half-day of the conference, plus I need to leave early tomorrow morning so she can get back."

"It's too bad you're missing the rest. I'll make sure to take great notes so you can use them later. Tomorrow will be easier. Mostly the wrap-up and Q&A."

"That would be great. Thanks, Lindsay." Emily took a drink of water to distract herself.

"If you don't mind me asking," Lindsay looked uncomfortable for a moment before proceeding, "where is the girls' dad this weekend?"

Emily coughed on the liquid that hadn't made it down her throat, and she quickly picked up her napkin and covered her mouth. Blake looked her way as she turned red and continued to half choke on both the water and the question.

Not making eye contact and dabbing at her mouth again to make sure she wasn't drooling, Emily coughed one last time. "He's … he was busy this week. Work needed him."

Blake eyed Emily suspiciously as she busied herself with her purse and coughed one more time. She didn't want to talk about Conrad tonight. She didn't want her professional life to have to mingle with her personal life.

Separate, she thought to herself, then shook her head as she realized just how hard she had been flirting and trying to gain Blake's attention.

"I think I might be ready to call it a night," Emily stated. She looked around the table, then settled a leveling look at Blake as she slid out of the chair. "Thank you for the invite. It was great to get to know you all a little better."

"Safe travels home, Emily," Jay said, extending a hand.

"You, too." Emily shook his hand, smiling and turned to Lindsay hugging her. She nodded at Blake and stepped away from the table. As she pulled her purse with her it caught on the chair at the next table and she stumbled. She felt a warm hand steady. She looked to see it was Blake's hand. His blue eyes considering her own. She stood, straightened herself, and smiled. "Thanks."

Blake nodded and released her arm. She tried not to sway toward the elevator as the effects of the wine took hold of her.

Emily angrily pressed her lips together as she realized the mistakes made over the last few hours. She fell back into her old habit of flirting without remorse.

"Fuck," she muttered under her breath.

She was embarrassed as she realized she was attracted to Blake. Though not like the way she was to Anika. She fell back into what was once comfortable for her.

The elevator opened and Emily stumbled in, not caring who saw her this time. She pressed the button for the third floor and leaned against the wall with her eyes closed. She heard the doors start to close, stop, then open again. When she opened her eyes, Blake was through the partially opened doors.

She stood up straight, "What floor?" she asked.

"Three," he replied, glancing at the lit panel, then looking intently at her. She pressed the close door button but didn't move her body from against the wall. She was aware of his natural muskiness and the light smell of his cologne. He still stared at her as the elevator reached the third floor and he indicated for her to step out first.

She hesitated, then mumbled a barely coherent thank you. As she stepped out, she tripped on the threshold and Blake caught her again. Emily blushed and tried to regain her composure, now more embarrassed than ever. She started to walk toward her room. Blake placed a hand around her waist to steady her.

Emily tried feebly to push him away, muttering that she was fine, but he continued to walk with her. She reached the door to her room and fumbled in her purse for the key. Blake stood intently, close in proximity to Emily's already flushed body. Having trouble finding her key, Blake reached to help, and Emily pulled away. Sighing, she took a deep breath, closed her eyes, and leaned against the door to her hotel room.

"I'm sorry, Blake," she began as she continued to search blindly for her key in the mess of her purse. "I know that I probably seemed to have led you on tonight, but I really need to go to bed."

Blake's eyes flashed with a combination of drink, frustration, and need. He placed his hand on the door, above Emily's head, and leaned closer, their faces inches apart.

"You flirted with me the entire conference. You've tried to get my attention, and now you have it." Blake stepped closer, their bodies almost touching. Emily's started into the unfamiliar blue of his.

"Blake …" Emily started, her stomach lurching into her throat. She tried to make her voice sound more confident than she felt. She tried to control of the shaking that threatened to overcome her body as she resumed her search of the key. She finally found it. "I'm really sorry. I know what it looked like."

"You're nothing but a fucking tease, then?" Face flush, he placed his other hand on her jaw. He forced her face up to his and pressed his body against Emily's

"Please, Blake. I'm sorry." Emily felt hot tears come to her eyes as at the same time regret and fear filled her mind and body. Unable to move her head, she could do nothing but stand there and fight back the tears threatening to make her weaker than she already seemed.

"This isn't what you were hoping for?" Blake asked sarcastically. He kissed Emily's cheek and took a deep breath. Then, pushing her head to the side, he whispered in her ear. "Isn't this what you were asking for?"

Emily started to cry, tears rolling down her face as his smell engulfed her senses and her mind went blank. Her body froze where it was. "No …," she replied quietly through squished lips.

"Is everything okay here?" A stern voice caused Blake to push violently away from Emily. Her head snapped sideways, and she winced in pain.

A woman in her sixties, ice bucket in hand, stared at them. She was in slippers and robe and had a firm but concerned look on her face as she took in the crying Emily and Blake's former stance.

He took a couple of steps away from Emily and smiled. "Everything is fine."

Emily made eye contact with the women and nodded as she slid her key card into the door and heard the click. Pulling the handle down to open the door, she slipped inside quickly. She saw the angry look on Blake's face as she closed it tightly and locked it.

She slid her back down the door and sat quietly as she heard the click of the door to the stairway and then sobbed hard into her knees.

She cried by the door for a long time. Eventually, the sobs subsided, and she tried to take a deep breath. Shakily, she took off her heels and threw them across the room. The fear and relief she had felt now changed to anger.

She shut her eyes and pressed her balled-up fists against them. Pushing up from the floor, she went to the bathroom. Leaning over the sink, she took a hard look at herself in the mirror.

Smeared eyeliner and ruined mascara ran down her cheeks and under her eyes. She shook her head and splashed cold water on her face. Turning around, she turned on the bath water hot.

Steam filled the bathroom. She pulled her shirt over her head, and the smell of Blake on it made her gag. Leaning over the toilet, the contents of her stomach expelled until there was nothing left. Dry heaves left her sore, and she cried some more as she hugged the toilet.

Eyes part open, Emily climbed into the bathtub and sunk deeply down. The hot water burned her skin, but she didn't care. The physical pain felt better than what was going on in her heart and head. She closed her eyes as she exhaled and dipped her head beneath the surface.

Flashbacks of the backseat of a car when she was eighteen mixed with the fresh thoughts of just moments ago. The memory of a similar smelling man on top of her made her sit up and gasp for air. She felt suffocated as she relived being beneath the person who forced himself in her. She cried as she released the pain from that long-ago night that had almost repeated itself.

She sobbed, but she opened her eyes. Her hands grasped the sides of the bathtub, eyes still unseeing, but her body remembered. Catching her breath, she leaned back again and fixated on a point on the ceiling, willing tonight to go away.

Washing her body gave her something else to concentrate on. She regretted not turning on music before she got in the bath.

After washing her hair and rinsing her body, Emily pulled a fluffy white towel from the rack. She stood in the tub and watched the water drain. She dried off, cleaned her face with lotion, and brushed her teeth.

Her tears felt miles away as she slowly settled into the familiar numb. Climbing into bed naked, she prayed sleep would come quickly and dreamlessly.

CHAPTER 7

Emily woke early. She rolled over as her sore body and queasiness brought back haunting memories from the previous night. She rushed to the toilet and dry-heaved as the events replayed in her mind. Shaking her head and splashing cold water on her face, Emily stared at her swollen jaw in the mirror.

Crying had made her eyes puffy, and there were faint bruises on her jaw and cheeks where Blake held her face. Her neck ached from his violent dismissal when he was discovered.

Tears came again. Emily fought them back with more cold water on her face. She started the shower, careful to make it not as hot as last night's bath. Her body had taken enough of a beating.

Feeling a little refreshed as she exited the shower, Emily quickly dressed then looked at her reflection. Her eyes were still a bit puffy, and she could see the fingerprint bruises. She took out her coverup and blended a thick layer over her face, paying special attention to the most sensitive areas.

She inspected herself before putting her toiletries away. Satisfied the obvious marks were hidden, Emily finished packing while sipping bitter hotel coffee. A knock shook her from her thoughts. She looked through the peephole. The hallway was empty. She scanned again, then quietly opened the door a crack, looking left, then right, then down. She bent down and opened the letter: it was an invoice for her stay.

Emily laughed nervously and left the room. Entering the parking lot, she fought back the urge to run to her SUV. The deserted parkade made her uncomfortable, and she wanted to be rid of the previous night's memories as quickly as possible.

***

"Mom!" Claire and Julia called in unison when Emily arrived three hours later. She barely made it through the door before they were both in her arms.

"I missed you girls so much!" she cried as she fought back tears for the third time that day. She hugged her girls tightly, then closed her eyes as she kissed their heads, one and then the other, repeatedly. "I love you. Were you good for Anika?"

"They were good, Emily. No worries on that at all." Anika stood, arms crossed over her chest and leaned against the wall. Emily stood and watched as Anika's face fell from the welcoming smile to a concerned frown. "Emily?" Anika started quietly, taking a step toward her.

"I'm okay," Emily whispered, unable to push back the tears any longer.

Anika took her into a tight, comforting embrace, and Emily buried her face in Anika's shoulder, sobs shaking her friend.

Her daughters watched in confusion.

"Mommy?" Claire asked, tugging on Emily's elbow, concerned.

"Your mom's okay," Anika responded unconvincingly. "She just needs a minute."

Emily took a deep breath and wiped at her tears. Turning to Anika she said, "Can you put some water on for tea?"

Anika nodded and turned toward the kitchen. Emily knelt beside the girls and took them in her arms again. "I'm so happy to see you, girls. Were you actually good?" Emily smiled and kissed their cheeks.

"We were good. Well, mostly good," Julia said matter-of-factly.

Emily laughed and raised an eyebrow, causing both girls to break into giggles. "Go play for a bit while I chat with Anika and find out how good you really were."

The girls ran off to their bedroom talking excitedly between each other. Emily watched them go then slowly made her way to the kitchen. She avoided Anika's eyes as she sat at the breakfast bar and toyed with a used crumb-filled napkin.

"Are you going to tell me what happened?" Anika's expression held tight with concern bordering on anger.

"It could have been worse …" Emily trailed off, poorly attempting a joke at the situation Anika knew nothing about yet.

"Emily …" Anika rolled her eyes. She turned off the stove and poured water into some fruity tea.

"I made a mistake." Emily shrugged her shoulders while Anika brought everything over. "I should have been more careful. I should have drunk less. I shouldn't have flirted like I did …"

Her shaking whisper could hardly be heard. She stared at the cupboard as more tears started to fall. Small puddles formed on her forearms.

"Emily…" Anika moved close to pull her into a hug. Emily sunk into Anika, her arms over her chest like a child needing to be protected, and quietly retold the previous night's events. Anika rubbed her back and hugged tighter when Emily's tears fell faster. Emily eventually pulled away and blew her nose on the crumbed napkin.

"I'm sorry." Emily looked down at the wet, soiled napkin in her lap.

"You have nothing to be sorry for!" Emily winced as Anika took her face to bring it eye-level. She kissed Emily's cheeks and jaw slowly, covering every sore, bruised area on her face.

"You didn't do anything wrong. You didn't deserve this. Know that! No matter what your actions were or how much you flirted, he had no right to do this."

Emily couldn't speak. She fell into Anika again and allowed herself the full release of emotions. Anika continued to hold her, stroking her back and whispering reassurances. Finally, Emily calmed enough to go to the bathroom and wash her face. Coming out, she saw Anika had gathered her bags at the door and was saying goodbye to Claire and Julia.

"I wish you didn't have to go." Emily stood in front of Anika. She straightened herself and hugged her chest into herself.

"I'm sorry, Emily." Tears welled in Anika's eyes as she embraced Emily, who again fell into Anika, but tears didn't fall this time. "I love you."

"I love you, Anika," Emily replied, hugging firmly then releasing Anika and wrapping her arms around herself again. Anika half smiled, nodded, and left as Emily held the door open for her. "Drive safely and let me know when you get home."

"I will."

Emily watched Anika walk down the hallway and around the corner to the elevator. She sighed as she closed and locked her apartment door. She could hear the girls playing together, their happy sounds reaching her ears and allowing her to smile.

CHAPTER 8

The music played in the background to drown out all but the girls' occasional raised voices on who should lead the next game. Claire and Julia each had a friend over and, despite there being four little girls in the 1000 square foot apartment, it was still relatively quiet.

Emily changed the song and started dancing to the beat of the music while she folded the mountain of laundry she avoided all week. She caught up on her work and other chores, so she had no more excuses.

While turning a pair of pants right side out, Emily's phone rang. Looking at the call display she saw it was Andrea.

"What are you up to tonight?" Andrea asked.

"I'm not sure, why?" Emily replied while she matched socks.

"Let's go out tonight. You've been working too hard lately, and I haven't had an evening away in months!"

"I don't know, Andrea. It's kind of short notice to find a babysitter ..."

"My sister is in town, and she's already offered to watch all the kids. She says we don't get out often enough. Her only request is we have drinks with her before we leave."

"I don't know –"

"Just say yes. You deserve to let loose, too," Andrea said, almost pleading with Emily to take a break from her busy life.

"Okay," Emily sighed. "What time should we be at your place?"

"Oh! Yay! Perfect! Come around four, and we can do dinner with the kids and get ready together as well."

Emily hung up and sat down. She didn't really feel like going out tonight, but she knew she needed to get her mind off work and the pieces she felt were missing in her life right now.

Emily and Anika's October weekend had left her drained and confused. Before then, she felt she had a good grasp on her life. She was concentrating on her girls and making headway at her new job. She didn't really miss the connection with another person, and the new friendships she made with a couple of coworkers and other moms was enough adult interaction to get her through the weeks and months.

Now, though, she found herself easily distracted throughout the day while the nights were frustrating moments of pleasuring herself and longing for someone to hold her. Someone to have in her arms and on her lips. Yet, Anika seemed so distant from her at the same time. She hadn't been returning her texts and emails as quickly. Emily found herself wishing she had almost listened to the voice she had silenced telling her to decline their weekend.

Grabbing the laundry basket, Emily went into the girls' bedroom to put their clothes away. "How would you like to go for a sleepover at Mackenzie's tonight?"

"Yay!" both girls jumped up and yelled in unison.

VANESSA M. THIBEAULT

"Andrea and I are going to go out for a bit tonight, but her sister Izzy will be there with you guys. Does that sound like fun?"

"Are you going to come back to sleep?" Claire asked looking up from the toy she was fidgeting with.

"Yes, sweetie. I'll only be gone a few hours, and you will be sleeping for most of it."

"Okay!" Claire smiled widely.

"Get together some clothes and a couple of toys if you want. We'll head over in about an hour after your friends are picked up, okay?"

"Okay, Mom," Julia replied and started to clean up the Legos all around them. "Help me, Claire."

The girls got to work cleaning with their friends, and Emily watched them for a few moments. The joy she often found in being able to be such a huge part of their lives overwhelmed her sometimes. It had a been a long journey so far. Conrad rarely tried to see them, not that it was so different than when they had all lived together. Unless they were at school, or the rare occasion they went to a friend's house, Emily never really got a break.

I do need a little time to myself, she thought as she left the girls' room. *Some time away and a few drinks will do me good.*

***

"I don't know about you," Izzy started, "but I can't wait for winter to be over."

"I agree! Too many stupid drivers with all this snow we've been having." Emily took a long swallow of Caesar and picked up her shot glass, "Cheers! To new friends and good times! Thanks for taking the kids tonight, Izzy."

"Cheers!" Izzy and Andrea picked up their shot glasses and downed the china white effortlessly.

"Should we call a cab?" Andrea asked, checking her phone for the time.

"Sounds good. I'll go up and say good night to the girls."

Emily walked up the steps of Andrea's three-story townhome to where the bedrooms were. Stopping at the top of the landing, Emily overheard the girls' conversation. "I don't have a dad," Emily heard Mackenzie say.

"Everyone has a dad," Claire replied.

"Well, I know that," Mackenzie said. "I mean, mine's just not here anymore. He didn't love my mom."

"My mom stopped loving my dad," Claire said angrily.

"No, Julia. Mom and Dad just couldn't get along anymore. When you can't get along you don't live together anymore," Julia said matter-of-factly. Though she was two years younger than Claire, the insight she had amazed Emily at times.

She was flabbergasted at their conversation. Her happy buzz evaporated as she listened to casual tone of these three children talking about such a serious situation.

"Sometimes people just stop loving each other. No big deal," Julia said.

"Sometimes I wish there was someone else there to help Mom." Claire's voice was sad.

"Nah. It's better, just you guys and her. You don't want anyone else taking her attention. You get her all to yourself this way," Mackenzie said quietly.

"Easy for you to say. You don't have a little sister," Claire said, the scowl clear in her voice. "At least when Dad was around there was someone else there, at least sometimes."

Emily decided she heard enough and continued down the hall. At the last minute, she decided not to mention that she heard their conversation. Now wasn't the time to bring up a painful discussion about absentee fathers and the truth behind why people get divorced.

"Hi girls." Emily knocked on the door and stuck her head in. "Andrea and I are getting ready to go. I just wanted to come up and say good night."

"Good night, Mom" Julia said a little sleepily. "I love you. Don't forget you're coming back to sleep with me."

"I won't, sweetie. Listen to Izzy. If you want to sleep up here with Mackenzie, you can do that, too. I will just be downstairs, okay?"

"Okay." Emily kissed Julia's cheek and brushed her fine hair out of her face.

"Be good for Izzy, okay Claire?"

"Of course, Mom," Claire hardly looked in Emily's direction and sounded annoyed.

"Claire." Emily moved in front of the TV, and Claire had no choice but to look at her.

"Yes, Mom." Claire made eye contact and reached out for a hug. "I love you."

"I love you too, sweetie."

"Good night, Mom."

"Have fun, Mackenzie."

"Thanks," Mackenzie replied, her eyes still on the TV.

Emily paused at the door and looked back at the three girls, sleepy and engrossed in their movie as though they hadn't been discussing anything before she came in. Turning, she just about ran into Andrea.

"Ready?" Andrea asked.

"Sure am," Emily replied. "When's the cab here?"

"About ten minutes. I'll meet you downstairs."

Emily went to the kitchen and poured herself another shot. She downed that one and decided to pour one more. Izzy came into the room as she picked up the bottle.

"Just topping off before you leave?" she asked. Emily was startled but regained her composure and resumed pouring.

"Join me for one before we go?" Emily stood straighter and handed a very full shot glass Izzy.

Izzy was the same age as Emily but didn't have an identical urge to settle down. She had shorter, curly blonde hair with dark red streaks.

She wore a pair of boyfriend jeans and a partially unbuttoned plaid shirt that showed a little of her chest. Small breasts curved out the shirt. Her slight waist and hips allowed it to hang comfortably just past the waist of her jeans.

Izzy didn't wear makeup on a typical day. She had dark eye lashes and light green eyes that seemed to hold laughter behind them.

She was the creative director at one of the publishing firms in downtown Vancouver. She'd started there as an intern, making coffee and staying far later than her pay covered to learn the ins and outs of the business. Now, nearly a dozen years later, she ran her own department.

In the six months she'd known Andrea, Emily had never seen Izzy with anyone. She always showed up to get-togethers and parties by herself, though she didn't seem perturbed or bothered by it at all. It seemed to fit her as naturally.

"Of course," Izzy replied, taking the glass. She held Emily's eye for a moment, hanging onto the shot for longer than necessary.

"To new and better," Emily stated quietly, not breaking eye contact.

"To new and better," Izzy agreed, clinking and downing the shot.

"Well, what about including me in the celebrations?" Andrea asked as her heels clicked on the tiled kitchen floor.

"Another round it is," Emily laughed and poured three more shots.

The three women cheered and set their shot glasses in the sink. The honking of the Uber didn't give time for any more of a conversation between the women.

"Thanks, Izzy," Andrea called as she walked out the door.

"Any time! Don't come home early! Take a cab home! Text me!" Izzy called after Andrea, smiling and leaning against the doorway.

Emily walked down behind Andrea and turned to look at Izzy. Something stirred in her. Izzy gave a little wave from her crossed arms and Emily smiled. Turning around, she quickened her pace and caught up to Andrea who was already directing the driver to where they needed to go.

CHAPTER 9

Andrea and Emily stepped out of the cab onto the slushy street and was greeted by the pounding bass of the club. The queue was about fifteen people long, so they strode to the back, wrapping their coats a little tighter around themselves and shoving their hands in their pockets.

Andrea talked excitedly about the club. "They're supposed to have one of the best DJs in the city."

"I haven't been out in so long, Andrea, I don't know if I even understand what that means any more." Emily laughed, wishing she had a drink. "Do they at least play decent music?"

"Of course!" Andrea laughed and leaned against Emily in an attempted hug without having to take her hands out of her pockets.

Emily removed one hand and gave Andrea's shoulder a squeeze. They laughed to themselves as the line moved two people up. Shifting their feet forward, Emily released Andrea and placed her hands back in her pockets.

"So, what's the deal with Izzy?" Emily inquired, "She seems like a great catch. Why doesn't she have a boyfriend?"

Andrea looked curiously at Emily and then laughed, "Boys aren't exactly her type."

Emily looked at Andrea, unsure for a moment what was meant. She furled her brow then glanced at Andrea again. "Oh!" Emily laughed at herself and turned pink.

"Dating women seems to be a bit tougher than finding men to date. She tries to keep her personal life on the down low, too. There have been a few women over the years, but no one has kept her attention. She seems to be pretty happy with her apartment and cat and career."

"That makes sense." Emily was embarrassed she hadn't caught onto the fact Izzy was a lesbian. Feeling silly and ignorant, she turned her attention to the queue ahead of them.

Eventually, a group of four men got into line behind her and Andrea. They were a little loud and boisterous but seemed to tone down once they got in the queue. They just laughed and joked quietly to themselves.

Andrea elbowed Emily and smiled as she glanced behind at the group of guys. Emily laughed and looked as well. One of them caught Emily's eye and nodded with a large smile on his face. His longer hair was styled to the side with just enough product to hold it in place but still make it look moveable. He had blue eyes and a day's worth of stubble. Emily could smell his musky aftershave from where she stood. All of them were dressed well with leather jackets, expensive shoes, and designer jeans.

Though there was the recognizable stirring from Emily as she smiled and looked away, she didn't feel a serious draw to him at all. She wanted the thrill of the chase and the flirting that would inadvertently occur, but that was it. The thought of crawling into bed with him and allowing his hands on her body turned her off immediately.

She shook her head as Blake's face flashed in her mind. Then she stepped forward to the chain the bouncer had just hooked back up.

Emily hadn't told Andrea about her relationship with Anika. There didn't seem to be a right time to tell. Plus, Emily wasn't sure how she would explain it. She hadn't decided how much she was willing to share with anyone or how much she even should.

She certainly didn't want to get Anika or Matisse in trouble with anyone or start any rumors, and she especially didn't want Matisse to get wind that her and Anika were still, or had been, seeing each other.

Andrea nudged Emily with her elbow to bring her back to the cold night and the buzz between Emily's ears. "Emily?"

"Yes?"

"This is Mike, Clint, Ryan and Kyle. They're out celebrating something about the law firm they work at," Andrea announced excitedly, the shots she drank at home clearly having taken effect. She bounced around a little to keep warm and smiled flirtishly. Then she gestured beside her. "This is Emily."

"Hi," Emily raised one hand from her pocket and smiled.

"I'm Clint," one man said as he reached his hand out to shake Emily's. He was the one who had smiled at her before.

Emily gave Clint's hand a shake and nodded with a smile. As the others introduced themselves, Clint continued to hold Emily's hand longer than necessary. She smiled and pulled it awkwardly from his. No one else seemed to notice the uncomfortable exchange, so they continued to make small talk as they waited for the bouncer to let them in.

"Do you guys all work –"

Emily was cut off by a crashing sound from the club's metal exit doors flinging open. Two guys, followed by three bouncers, came falling out. The pair of women behind them screamed and yelled incoherently.

Emily instinctively stepped back from the scene and tripped over a pile of snow that collected next to a streetlamp. Leaning back, she flailed her arms out to steady herself against something. At the last second, Clint caught her.

"Thanks," Emily said. The smell of his cologne filled her senses, and she felt her stomach churn. Grabbing onto the lamp post, it took her a moment to fully right herself again. She awkwardly shook Clint off her arm and gained her composure.

"Not tonight, Adam!" one of the bouncers yelled after the men as they stumbled back from the doors and fingered the bouncers. Clint turned his head to the scene unfolding before them. Emily noticed his jaw clench.

"Fuck you, too," one of them men yelled back, kicking at the snow.

"Let's just get out of here," one of well-dressed women said as she shrugged her coat on and jabbed a finger down the street, taking them directly passed Emily and her end-of-line group.

Emily turned and the doorman looked at her, then looked back at Clint. "Ladies," he said, holding the chain open for them. Emily grabbed Andrea by the arm and lead her through the opening.

"Thank you," Emily said, giving the man a nod as he deliberately closed the chain behind them, leaving the four men waiting outside in the cold.

Andrea looked back with a smile and wave. She began to say something while Emily pulled her through the door and toward the coat check.

"What was that about?" Andrea looked annoyed and shook herself from Emily.

"Those guys were giving me a creepy vibe."

"You just haven't been out in a while." Andrea shrugged out of her coat, straightened her blouse, and threw her purse over her shoulder. "They seemed like decent guys, and it's not like they're going to come home with us or anything."

Emily sighed and exchanged their coats with the check woman., Then she grabbed Andrea's hand, "I don't want any drama tonight. Not with men. Let's have fun, okay?"

Andrea squeezed back and pulled Emily enthusiastically toward the bar. "Let's get a drink."

Pushing their way through the already growing crowd, Emily and Andrea finally made it to the bar. "Two china whites, a double honey jack and a double gin tonic," Emily ordered for both her and Andrea. Pulling out cash from her wallet, Emily dropped her purse in the process. Stooping to pick it up, a woman with large brown eyes and long brunette hair stopped to help her as well.

"Thanks," Emily said loudly hoping to be heard over the music.

"No problem." The woman smiled and leaned up against the bar. Holding up two fingers, as she caught the bartender's eye, two Coronas were quickly placed in front of her.

Emily pointed to her china whites and ordered another, pointing to the lady. The three women clinked their glasses together and downed the cinnamon and chocolate liquid. The brunette nodded, smiled, then walked away. Emily watched her go, aroused by her long legs in calf high boots and skinny jeans.

Andrea pointed to a table at the far end of the bar, farther away from the blasting music. Emily nodded and they gingerly made their way through dancing couples and giggling packs of younger women who you could hardly call more than girls.

"How's your drink?" Emily asked Andrea, trying to make small talk. Her buzz had been killed for the second time that night, and she desperately needed to feel free and loose.

She downed half her honey jack and leaned back in the booth. She let the music take her with it for the moment.

"It's good. You look like you need another?"

Emily nodded, not bothering to open her eyes. She concentrated on the beat of the music and didn't hear when Andrea ordered them more drinks. Andrea was kind enough to let Emily come down and find her peace with the evening. She was sensitive enough to Emily to know how her anxiety affected her sometimes. Emily was appreciative of the need to not make small talk for a few minutes.

She sensed someone close to their table and opened her eyes, Emily saw Clint and his friends at the bar as the waitress brought over their drinks. Two more china whites each plus Andrea ordered her a beer. Andrea followed Emily's gaze and kicked her friend under the table.

"We'll be careful," Andrea said. "Lets just have a little fun tonight. No harm can come from just dancing."

Emily looked her. She wanted to have a good time and pretend that they were other people for the night. Forget about the kids and all their responsibilities for the time being.

Emily rolled her eyes and pushed her gut feelings aside, "Okay … fine! But we don't leave each other, right?"

Andrea waved a hand high in the air. "Got it!" she confirmed enthusiastically.

Mike waved and tapped Clint on the shoulder. He made eye contact with Emily and smiled, nodding. Paying for their drinks, they made their way over to the women.

"Nice to see you guys finally made it in," Andrea said

"Yeah, the bouncer was being a bit of a dick," Clint said.

"He told us to behave ourselves before he let us in." Ryan laughed and took a long pull on his beer. He was short, but stocky, maybe only two inches taller than Emily, with dirt blonde hair left to grow a little longer than his ears.

The ladies moved together in the middle of the bench to allow room for the four guys. Emily wasn't happy about this lack of control and an exit plan, but Andrea seemed to be just fine with sitting close to Mike. Clint scooted closer to Emily. She smiled and placed her hand on her drink, her other on her purse next to Andrea.

Andrea glanced over as Emily's hand brushed her side, and she gave her a smile and a nod toward Clint. Emily rolled her eyes and turned to make small talk with him until the server showed up with a tray full of shots.

"Tequila for everyone!" Kyle exclaimed loudly pointing to the tray. The shots were unloaded, at least two for everyone, along with a saltshaker and a bowl of limes.

"To nights out!" Andrea called, sprinkling salt on her hand and putting her shot in the air.

Everyone cheered loudly. Emily skipped the salt and lime, looked straight at Clint, and downed her shot easily. The alcohol warmed her, and she felt herself loosen up and get her buzz back. Another couple of shots and Emily was happily laughing at the jokes the guys were making and the funny stories they had about some of the screw ups they had to cover up for the partners back at the firm they worked at.

"I love this song!" Andrea exclaimed and nearly jumped out of her seat, "Let's go dance!"

Emily laughed and nudged Clint in the ribs playfully. "Let's go!" she said, wiggling closer to indicate she wanted to get out. They all made their way to the dance floor. Emily kept a close eye on Andrea but was having plenty of fun herself. It felt good to let go, to let loose and forget the stress of the kids, Conrad and even Anika.

Emily allowed Clint to run his hands over her hips and dance dangerously close, though she still mostly kept her distance. Once again, the familiar stirring of a man close to her made her question her resolution, but the unease she still felt about her feelings and the evening kept him at arms length.

The song ended, and Emily looked around for Andrea. Spotting her at the bar, she went over, "Hey! We were supposed to be staying together!"

"Sorry! The song was almost over, and I needed another beer."

"No worries, but let's go to the bathroom."

"I'll be right back," Andrea flirted with Mike as she grabbed her purse and beer and let Emily lead her from the bar.

The quiet of the bathroom was deafening with only muted base being heard. "Are you having fun?" Emily asked Andrea as the shared the stall.

"Yes. Mike seems super nice. He's already asked if he can see me again."

"You're still coming home with me tonight, Andrea."

"Oh, I know that, Emily. I have no interest in one-night stands with Mackenzie. It's not worth the risk of having her hurt. But it sure is fun to have something new in my mind for later when I'm alone."

"Isn't that the truth!" Emily laughed at Andrea's raised eyebrow and mock sexiness. Looking at Andrea, eye lids starting to get a little droopy and not quite as steady on her heels Emily asked, "Are you ready to get going soon?"

Andrea glanced at her phone, "It's only one. Let's stay for a couple more drinks then call a cab. Maybe another hour?" she questioned, almost pleadingly with a smile plastered on her face.

Emily flushed and rolled her eyes at Andrea, "A couple more drinks. We still have kids to look after tomorrow!"

"True. That's one thing I'm sure Izzy ISN'T looking forward to if we're not home soon," Andrea laughed as did Emily at the thought of Izzy disheveled and trying to organize breakfast for the three kids at seven in the morning.

Going back to the bar to refresh their drinks, Clint and Mike waited for them with new shots lined up. Emily looked at Andrea who shrugged her shoulders and sauntered up to Mike with a big smile on her face. Emily smiled reservedly at Clint and took her place between him and Andrea. Clint put his hand around her waist as they clinked once again and downed their shots.

The alcohol caught up with Emily, and she found herself stumbling a little on the dance floor. Clint was quick to catch her when a stray elbow knocked her sideways and spilled a drink on her. The beat of the music slowed down, and Clint didn't let go after she regained her balance.

Unsure how to get herself out of this, Emily succumbed to the desire of needing to be in someone's arms. The pit of her stomach growled at her, but she ignored it for the old comfort of musky cologne and strong arms – a heartbeat under her cheek.

The song changed again, and Emily pulled, feeling guilty for allowing her shameful primal loneliness and yearning for familiar territory to overwhelm her real desires and needs. Clint caught her ass in his hand and cupped it roughly, pulling Emily closer into him. He pushed her chin up towards his, and Emily stood frozen for a moment before her head caught up with her body.

"Get off me!" She pushed him away from her with the understanding she was probably over-reacting a touch. However, she didn't care She wanted to exert her guilt and confusion physically. Plus, the alcohol was also playing a role, "Just because I dance with you doesn't mean you can put your hands all over me!"

Emily turned to Andrea and Mike. "Time to go," she said as she led her friend away from the dance floor. With a confused glance at Mike who stood there looking dumbfounded, she stumbled behind. Gaining her footing by the time they were at the coat check, Andrea shook Emily off, "What is going on?!"

"I just think it's time to go."

Andrea gave Emily a glare and crossed her arms defiantly. "What happened?" she asked concerned, drunk, and pissed off.

"Clint decided it was time to play grab ass and try to kiss me. I'm not interested in it." Emily sighed in anger, as she exchanged their tickets for their coats.

"Emily … we've all had more than just a little to drink … maybe you're overreacting …" Andrea trailed off as Emily glared at her and walked into the brisk January air.

As she called for a cab, she continued to walk half a block down so as not to be right in front of the club.

"I'm not overreacting."

"Emily –"

"Whatever happened to gentlemen … and to asking …" Emily shook her head, "I don't think this scene is for me anymore. I expect too much."

"I'm sorry Emily—"

The cub door banged shut. They turned and saw Mike and Clint look both ways, searching for Andrea and Emily.

"Shit …" Emily muttered under her breath, straightening up and proceeding to look down the street in search of the cab.

"Emily!" Clint called, half jogging toward them. Emily ignored the advance and stepped toward the street, looking once again for the elusive cab.

"Emily …" Clint started again as he reached her and stopped about a meter beside her. "I thought you were into it. We were dancing and …" Clint drunkenly swayed his hips in mock dancing, laughing.

"You know, I'm just not into anything one-night standish, so good night." Emily turned her back and hopefully looked down the street a third time Andrea stumbled, and Emily caught her with her arm around her waist.

"Maybe you'd rather just fuck your girlfriend then," Clint laughed with his buddies, thinking he was funny. Mike looked uncomfortable and offered an apologetic look and a shrug of his own intoxicated shoulders.

"You know what? Maybe I don't do dick because of guys like you."

The cab finally arrived, and Emily ushered Andrea in first. She got in next and went to close the door. Clint blocked her and stooped down. His hard breath, sick with drink and yearning, stuck to Emily.

"Dykes still want dick, Emily …"

Emily gave him a shove and closed the door. She gave the driver the address, and they left Clint, Mike and the others that had joined them stumbling on the sidewalk.

Andrea waved at Mike, and he waved back with a boyish grin. Leaning back against the seat, Emily realized just how inebriated she and Andrea were.

***

The ride was about thirty minutes. By the time Emily paid the cab driver, she realized Andrea was passed out. She tried to wake Andrea as she pulled her out of the cab and started up the steps. Struggling with how out of it she was, Emily was relieved to find Izzy soon by her side to help her sister up the stairs and into the townhouse.

They got her up the stairs and in her bedroom. Combining efforts, they removed Andrea's boots and coat and laid her comfortably under her covers. Emily undid her hair and pulled the covers up close to her face where it could be warm and comforting.

Emily and Izzy looked at each other and giggled on the way out as they carefully and quietly closed the door.

"How was the night?" Izzy asked as they made their way downstairs. Although Emily's mind was fairly clear, she still stumbled and needed to hold the railing for support. Noticing Emily's careful steps, Izzy added with laugh, "I see you had a good time."

Emily laughed, shook her head, and stumbled. Finding her footing, she found herself on the couch while Izzy disappeared into the kitchen. Emily closed her eyes for a moment thinking about how the evening had played out. Shaking her head once again, she sat up as Izzy came in the room with two mugs.

"Tea?" Izzy asked, setting a hot cup of Earl Grey down in front of Emily with milk and sugar in it.

"Thanks," Emily tucked her legs under her and picking up the warm mug. Breathing in its aroma, she sighed, "Is it just me, or does it seem like men never grow up?"

"It's not just you," Izzy laughed. "Why do you think I like women?"

"Biology?" Emily teased back and laughed. Izzy sat next to Emily on the small couch, one leg under her as she leaned against a corner. She placed her other leg on the coffee table in front of her.

"I don't think I'm into the club scene anymore. I hadn't need to one in a while. I forgot how terrible drunk guys are. I think Andrea got a phone number, though." Emily rolled her eyes.

"If she can find it in the morning." Izzy snorted and sipped her tea. They sat in silence, the warm glow of the lamp and soft beiges in the living room lent to a cozy feeling. Their teas were almost done.

"Thank you for watching the kids tonight," Emily said quietly as she placed her empty mug on the table and shifted, stretching her legs out.

"No problem. They're great kids, Emily, really."

"Thanks," Emily replied, looking at Izzy. She saw the other woman studying her. Emily found herself blushing and laughed, waving her hand in the air, "When are you going to have some of your own? You'd make a great mom."

"Oh, I think I'm good just playing the fun aunt who doesn't have to get up early EVERY morning," Izzy tilted her head back and stretched with her arms out. Emily followed the line of her jaw with her eyes. Her neck was slim and, once again, Emily could see the small rises of her breasts under her shirt.

She hadn't changed from earlier, but one more button had been undone. Emily shifted closer to Izzy. The warmth of their legs, now pressed together, sent tingles up Emily. Izzy returned from her stretch and looked at Emily.

Emily reached for a small piece of fuzz that was stuck to Izzy's pants. Emily wanted to touch Izzy, to feel her warmth. She suddenly missed Anika. Rather, she missed the times they had spent together in her bed, warm and full of love and desire. Naked warm bodies. Smooth skin and gentle caresses.

"I should go to bed," Emily started, getting up from the couch. "The kids will be up in like three hours."

"Good night, Emily," Izzy replied, standing up to embrace her.

Emily hugged her back tightly, and then they stood there for a few moments. Emily took in the sensation of Izzy's body pressed to hers. Her small frame, though they were similarly sized, didn't seem small. They released each other slowly and Emily found Izzy's mouth with hers. It was a slow kiss, their lips tentative.

"Emily," Izzy started. "You're drunk."

"I'm sorry," Emily apologized, pulling back. "I shouldn't have …"

"Don't be sorry, but I don't want you to do something you might regret later." Izzy held Emily's hand. "We can talk tomorrow."

"Sure," Emily felt embarrassed and rejected. Not meeting Izzy's eyes, she turned to go when Izzy pulled her close and kissed her.

"Emily. It's not that I don't want to, but just not tonight," Izzy whispered and kissed Emily again. Her hand around the back of Emily's neck, the other still in Emily's. "Good night."

"Good night," Emily replied, as Izzy walked out of the room. She sat on the couch and put her head between her hands. She was suddenly dizzy and overwhelmed. Deciding that the couch was a good place to sleep, Emily pulled the fuzzy blanket off the back and curled up on her side. It didn't take her long to fall asleep.

CHAPTER 10

"Mom … Mom … Mom…" Julia whispered in Emily's ear. "Mom … I'm hungry."

Emily moaned and squinted her eyes open at her daughter. Moving to a sitting position, she immediately regretted the number of shots she had done the night before. Her head pounded as a reminder, and her body ached from dancing in heels all night and sleeping squished on the couch.

"Is anyone else up?"

"I dunno. Maybe."

Emily closed her eyes to calm her now upset stomach. She was going to have to get her headache under control if she had any hope of keeping any food down this morning to feel better.

"Go check the kitchen, I think I hear someone in there," Emily instructed. "Can I have a water, please?" she called to Julia as she ran out of the living in search of food.

Emily leaned back on the couch and stretched her legs on the coffee table. She pulled the blanket over her as thoughts of last night flashed across her mind: shots, dancing, some guy kissing her, and total overreaction.

Then she kissed Izzy, and she kissed her back. Emily groaned as that embarrassing moment set in, but she also felt a tingle of excitement.

"Emily?"

Emily had drifted off into her head and pain and didn't hear Izzy come into the room. She sat up and drowsily looked up at Izzy standing in the doorway of the living room in a long night shirt with the words 'sleep tight' printed in cursive and surrounded by stars. The pink highlighted the same color in her cheeks, and her hair was a mess of sleep and uncaring.

"Emily?" Izzy asked again.

"Yeah," Emily replied, groggily hungover, her head still spinning.

"Would you like some coffee?"

"Yes, please," Emily replied putting her head between her hands. "Maybe some water, too, please?"

"Sure thing." Izzy smiled, watched Emily for another moment, then left.

Emily groaned out loud and stood, steadying herself on the edge of the couch. She gently walked to the bathroom. When she returned to the couch, Izzy was there with her coffee and water.

"I brought you something for your headache, too," Izzy placed two ENO tablets next to the water. "And something for your stomach."

"Thank you." Emily looked up at Izzy who, again, studied her with curiosity. Emily met the gaze with the same feeling mixed with embarrassment. "I'm sorry for last night."

"There's nothing to be sorry for," Izzy sat next to Emily on the couch. "I kissed you back, remember?"

Emily nodded. She did remember, and the thought of their lips pressed together, Izzy's hand on the back of her neck, made warmth flow through her.

"Do you want to go for coffee later?" Emily asked, taking the leap. Knowing the path she had been following hadn't been being true to who she was, she was curious to explore this nagging part of her. The part that said she wasn't happy with men, she wasn't happy with who she had been with in the past. The part that kept reminding her of Anika and kept drawing her back.

"I'd love to have a cup of coffee with you." Izzy put a hand on Emily's leg. "Now and later." Izzy picked up her mug of coffee and sipped it. Emily picked hers up and took a tentative sip, not wanting to burn her mouth.

"I'd like that."

Julia and Claire burst into the room a few minutes later, fully dressed and filled with energy. "Can we watch a movie today? Can we play with play dough? Can Mackenzie come to our house?"

"Slow down!" Emily said, finding the noise excruciating. "Is Mackenzie's mom up yet?"

"No, but I'm sure she would be fine with it," Mackenzie piped up in response.

"I think I'm going to take the girls home soon so they can get their homework done," she looked at Mackenzie, "and I think you need to do yours as well. Let your mom sleep for a while longer. Girls, go get your stuff together and help tidy up. We're going to leave in a bit."

"Aww, mom!" the girls whined in unison.

"We have stuff to do at home. Let's go! Or there's no TV later." The kids stomped off to do what they were told.

"You're a good mom," Izzy stated as she held her mug with both hands. She moved her foot to casually caress Emily's in reassurance.

"Thank you," Emily managed in a small voice. She wasn't thinking about the kids. The closeness of Izzy and the deliberate attempt to comfort and reassure with physical touch distracted her. "How does three for coffee sound?"

"It sounds great."

Emily finished her coffee and got up, "Are you done?"

Izzy looked up, green eyes meeting Emily's blue ones. Emily got lost in the flickering, changing colors and found herself frozen. Izzy smiled and, for once, blushed. Emily often doubted herself, but here she believed the feelings she was experiencing were reflected. Instead of giving Emily her cup, Izzy put her hand in hers, stood, and took the cups.

"I'll see you at three." Izzy stepped past Emily, her bra-free breasts brushing against Emily's arm as she walked by.

Emily ran her hands through her messy hair and reached in her pocket for a hair tie. Tying it back, she gathered her belongings, put them in the car, then went back in the house to call the girls. "Julia! Claire! Time to go, guys!"

Surprisingly, they both came bounding down and put on their boots and coats on without a fight. Mackenzie came trailing down, "Don't forget to call mom later so I can come visit, too!"

"Get your mom to call me when she finally finds her way out of bed," Emily laughed and gave Mackenzie a one-armed hug. "Come on, girls. Say thank you to Izzy and bye to Mackenzie." The girls did what their mother asked, and they were soon out the door.

***

The drive home was quiet. They were all tired and happy to get back to their cozy apartment. Coming in the door, Emily dropped her purse, and the girls left their coats and boots scattered. Emily didn't bother to nag about picking anything up. She ushered the girls into her room and turned on *Beauty and the Beast*. With all three of them together, Emily drifted off into a light sleep.

She woke to the DVD's home screen music repeating itself. She rolled over and looked at the clock. *Two o'clock. Crap.* Emily sat up and followed the sound of the girls out to the kitchen. "Why didn't you guys wake me up?"

"You looked cozy," Claire replied as she spread cream cheese on a slightly mutilated bagel in front of her. The cupboard was littered with dishes, crumbs, apple slices, utensils, and other random items.

They had decided to make their own lunch which consisted of cream cheese bagels, apple slices, dried cranberries, and milk. They had their plates out and each had a chair and an apparent job in the way of making lunch. On the adjacent counter was a tray laid out with a mug of tea which didn't appear to have been made with hot water, two notes and roughly cut apple slices.

"Mom! You're not supposed to be looking!" Julia exclaimed as she saw her mother's eyes raking over the mess in the kitchen.

"Be careful with the knife," Emily cautioned. "I'm going for a shower. And I'm not peeking!" Emily winked at Julia and, giving them both kisses and ignoring the mess, she relished in the hot shower.

The warm water fell over her naked body and Emily thought back to Izzy once again. She was only the second woman she had ever kissed, and it excited her. Her lips had been soft and inviting and she had smelled like spicy vanilla. The way she had pulled Emily closer to reassure her that she wanted to talk more about this made Emily realize that there might be people like her out there. Ones who wanted more than one-night stands and hidden relationships.

Emily got out of the shower. After drying her hair, she wrapped her towel around her and exited the bathroom to go get dressed. She could hear Julia and Claire laughing and a voice she couldn't make out talking and laughing with them.

"Girls?" Emily called peeking around the corner, "Who are you talking to?"

"Izzy's here, Mom," Claire called out, laughing again.

Emily stopped in her tracks as she came around the corner. Izzy sat on the couch with both girls near her.

Claire was trying to see what Izzy had in her hand. Julia sat close to Izzy and watched with a smile on her face as Izzy tricked Claire once again.

"Hi, Emily," Izzy didn't look up immediately – she continued to concentrate on the trick she played with the girls. When she did look up and saw Emily standing in her towel, a mix of surprise, appreciation and embarrassment crossed her face.

"Hi," Emily said, hugging the towel closer to her. "I'll … just go get dressed."

Izzy smiled and nodded,

her attention pulled by the girls as Emily turned in search of clothes. Trying not to stress over what she should wear, she settled on a pair of black leggings and an oversized, knit sweater. Running a brush quickly through her hair and putting some lotion on her face, Emily came out still rubbing the lotion onto her hands.

Izzy now stood in the kitchen, the girls having dragged her in to show their latest artwork on the fridge. Emily leaned against the kitchen doorway for a few moments and watched the three of them. Izzy pointed and asked questions about the pictures and schoolwork plastered over the fridge. Julia and Claire excitedly answered. Izzy smiled and laughed with the girls while they described their school days and hopes for the next week.

Emily smiled. It had been a long time since anyone had interacted with Julia and Claire like that beside her. Their dad never did, they had no family around and Anika was miles away. She appreciated the way Izzy made eye contact with each girl and the way she redirected them when they started to bicker.

"Hey," Emily finally said, coming in to put away the snacks and dishes the girls had left all over the counter. "Are you girls talking Izzy's ears off?"

"Izzy said she'll come to our school concert in February," Claire exclaimed excitedly jumping around Emily's legs and reaching up for a hug. Emily squeezed her close with one arm and turned to put the milk back in the fridge.

"That's really exciting! Remember that she might have to work though, okay?"

Emily made eye contact with Izzy. Her hair was a little tamer than it had been this morning, but her face was still clear from make up. Her brightly patterned leggings hugged her slight curves and a white, V-neck t-shirt fell loose off her breasts. Emily smiled as Izzy ruffled Julia's hair.

"Girls? Why don't you go and play? Izzy and I are going to talk for a bit, okay?" Emily coaxed as she came around the counter to turn on the kettle.

"Mom ..." Claire complained, slumping over.

"You can show Izzy some more of your school stuff after, okay?"

Izzy laughed as Julia and Claire didn't respond and instead ran off in search of something else to place their attention. "You have beautiful girls, Emily."

"Thank you," Emily replied quietly as she continued to tidy the kitchen up. "Do you want a cup of coffee or tea? Or a glass of wine?"

"Coffee would be great. Thanks."

"You can sit if you want." Emily pointed to the breakfast bar stools with a wooden spoon she was putting away in the jar. Taking out a French press, Emily snuck a look at Izzy. She was studying Emily again, which made her blush as their eyes met. "Sorry for the mess. I let the girls make their own lunch today and ... well ..."

Both women looked around and giggled at the crumbs, dirty utensils and other odd things spread around the cupboards. Turning to the fridge, Emily removed the creamer and placed it beside two large hand-crafted mugs on the bar. "How was the rest of your morning? What time did Andrea finally get up?"

"It was good. Mackenzie worked on her homework and helped me tidy up. Andrea got up around one and still wasn't feeling great. You were right, though. She was gushing about that Mike. I told her to be safe and take someone with her if she was going to meet him."

"I'm glad she had fun. Mike seemed okay, but you never know when you meet someone at the club."

"True."

Caught in their thoughts, they were silent as Emily poured coffee. The girls could be heard playing a game in their room, occasionally raised voices of frustration drifting out, but they seemed to solve their quarrels quickly today.

"I'm sorry about last night." Emily was still embarrassed, yet she was also intrigued that Izzy sat with her today.

"You have nothing to be sorry for. Like I said before, I kissed you back, remember? I was surprised … I really had no idea. I just thought you were divorced and taking your time to concentrate on your daughters and career."

"Well …" Emily started. Her elbows were on the counter and she faced the cupboards, coffee mug in her hands. She chewed on her bottom lip for a moment, thinking of Anika, "No one here knows this, but before I moved, before my marriage ended, I had a relationship with a good friend of mine. We kept it a secret for almost four years until I moved. She left me with a lot of questions that, I guess, looking back now …" Emily searched for a way to put her thoughts into words. "They were questions I had tucked down inside me for a very long time. It was our relationship that was the catalyst for me ending my marriage. It wasn't our relationship that was the issue, but that she finally made me realize how I deserved to be treated."

"What happened with you and –"

"Anika."

"What happened with you and Anika?" Izzy asked

"Well … there were a lot of other things that made our relationship complicated. So, in the end, she decided that it was important to make things with her husband work, for the sake of her career and children."

Emily found herself tearing up at the thought of Anika. Talking about her to someone else brought back a flood of emotion. Giving life to the words she had been holding onto for so long left her with the longing of unfinished business and questions. Shaking her head and closing her eyes for a moment to hide the tears, Emily took a large gulp coffee.

"I'm sorry, Emily." Izzy reached to place her hand over Emily's on the edge of her cup. Emily held Izzy's hand, allowing them to settle on the counter between them.

"It's okay. I mean, it's been difficult, and the girls loved her like an aunt, but we both had to do what we needed to do for our families. A long-distance thing would have been really hard."

"It's hard when kids are involved. I've been there." Izzy sighed and leaned her chin on her hand. "Not the last woman I was seeing, but the one before had two kids from a previous relationship. She had so much baggage left and unresolved issues that it ended up affecting the relationship. Kids totally change the game."

"So, on that note … Where does that leave us?" Emily didn't want either one of them to waste their time if they didn't want to explore these feelings further. She didn't want to drag her heart through the pain of falling for someone again, only to find out they hadn't felt the same at all, hadn't had the same intentions, needs or desires. She wanted to be sure this was a good fit for them, and, most importantly, potentially for her daughters.

"I'm not sure …" A troubled look came over Izzy's face. She opened her mouth to speak, them closed it. "I've … felt an attraction to you since we first met, but I thought it was only on my end and something that would never materialize as I definitely thought you were straight."

"I've felt something toward you as well but wasn't really looking for anything. This is all new to me. I don't know how to go about recognizing if a woman is into me or not. I wanted to concentrate on my girls and get settled with our new home, and school, and my job …" Emily quickly rattled off the feelings in her heart and a few of the million thoughts rushing across her mind. "I have a lot of baggage. The girls have a lot of baggage, and not just with Anika. We all have a lot of healing to do from Conrad. We will probably be healing our entire lives because he keeps hurting us."

Izzy squeezed Emily's hand. "It's okay. We all have baggage, and I have no intention on being intrusive on your life."

"I'm sorry. I'm all over the place. I know I overthink and jump far too far ahead sometimes."

"Let's start here, right now, with these cups of coffee. I'd love to get to know you better, but I think we both agree we need to take things slow."

"That sounds wonderful," Emily smiled. Placing her cup on the counter she swiveled her chair to face Izzy and leaned over to embrace her.

CHAPTER 11

Emily clumsily followed the yoga instructor's movements on TV as she tried to keep her balance. Thirty minutes in and she was sweating.

I need to workout more. Emily thought as she fell against her couch in frustration. Noting there was less than five minutes left in the workout, she slumped to the floor and began stretching slowly as she used the remote to change the channel to some music.

Laying flat on her back, she let the notes fill her mind and allowed her body to relax. She let her mind wander, and she found herself thinking about Izzy. A smile built as she remembered how Izzy's lips had felt when they had said goodbye the night before. Emily wanted so much more than that one kiss, but she knew it was important for the two of them to take things slowly.

Izzy ended up staying for dinner, even though she'd only intended on coming for coffee. They spent the afternoon laughing and getting to know one another. Izzy helped Emily with the girls when it was bedtime and they'd shared the clean up from dinner. Neither of them seemingly minding the chores.

Once the girls were settled, the pair sat on the couch, drank tea, and talked for hours. It was close to midnight when they finally looked at the clock.

Emily was disappointed to see Izzy go, but she reassured her that they would get together soon. Emily had smiled and leaned in for a hug with Izzy. She was pleasantly surprised when Izzy kissed her. It was as though she had sensed the Emily's trepidation about the evening's end and knew the perfect way to reassure her.

Izzy's lips had been soft, not as hungry as Anika's. Emily had always felt as though their lips were parched and would die without one another. On the other hand, Izzy's mouth had been confident and patient. Holding on just long enough to remind Emily she could be excited still. She had hugged herself in bed that night, feeling full instead of lonely. It had been a long time since Emily hadn't felt lonely. It allowed her to have one of the best sleeps in a long time.

Emily got off the floor and stripped on her way to shower before leaving to go get groceries. Soon enough, she was navigating traffic to the Costco.

She walked by a mother with three young kids in her cart and felt a pang of time lost. Costco was a lot more enjoyable now that she didn't have to take two screaming kids with her. She could look at what she was buying instead of rushing through the store and hoping she hadn't forgotten anything. But she still missed those days with the girls. Things had certainly been simpler. Rather, the information she'd needed to share with the girls had been simpler. They didn't need to know as much, and they didn't have as many questions either.

Emily smiled at the overwhelmed mom and picked up the stuffed bear the youngest had thrown to the ground for probably the thirtieth time that day. "You're doing a great job. It's hard, but you'll miss it one day." Emily didn't wait for the mother to respond. She pushed her cart away with tears in her eyes. The time went too fast, and now she was worried she may lose her daughters.

She mused over how frustrating the strained relationship between the girls and Conrad still was. She gave him all of her and more, and he didn't have the decency to support her decision to better herself and the family. He didn't even have the balls to call and ask her to rethink the custody.

He had done, as usual, whatever he wanted to do because it was going to benefit him. Trying to take the girls from her had nothing to do with what was best for them; it had everything to do with his ego and pride and the beating they had taken since Emily left.

Shaking her head as she picked up a bag of peas and three containers of raspberries, she saw a familiar face that stopped her in her tracks. Standing near the cheese display was Matisse, Anika's husband. Emily froze, debating whether she should hide behind a display of oranges or acknowledge that she had seen him.

Before she could decide, he looked up and met her eye. His face lit with recognition, and he pushed his cart toward her. She moved out of the middle of the aisle as she heard someone clear their throat behind her. Her face flushed and her heart raced as she struggled to stay calm and casual.

"Emily!" Matisse called as he closed in. He reached out to hug her. Emily kept one arm on her cart as she reluctantly returned the hug.

"Matisse! What are you doing here? You know there are closer Costco's to where you live, right?" Emily joked.

"I'm down here for work and headed home later tonight. I decided to do a quick shop for Anika while I was down here. She's been so busy with the kids and her school stuff."

"That's fair. How's she been? Besides busy, of course. I haven't talked to her in a while."

Emily felt a pang of regret and confusion thinking about Anika. She missed her friend, but something had changed. It hurt and confused her, making her wonder what was going on.

"Just busy. You know the twins. Anika has her hands full."

"Yes, I sure do. Well –"

"Do you want to grab lunch after this? I don't have to be back at the office until three."

"Um …" Emily hesitated.

It was hard enough with everything going on with Conrad, let alone the past that Matisse and she had, but it was nice to see a familiar face. Emily had tried to push the mistake she had made being a part of Anika and Matisse's marriage out of her mind.

She didn't want to have to think about how he had hurt Anika, how he had forced the choice for both women. Maybe he could shed some insight into what was going on with Conrad. If nothing else, she wasn't eating lunch alone today. "Sure. There's a Moxie's at the other end of the parking lot. Meet there in about an hour?"

"Sounds good." Matisse left it at that, and Emily stood for a moment longer, suddenly feeling weighted at having agreed to lunch. "Ugh," she muttered under her breath as she pushed her cart through the throngs of people to quickly finish her shopping. She'd had the rest of her shop to think about lunch and Matisse. She still wasn't completely sure what his angle was for this, but she knew it wasn't as innocent as he made it out to be.

***

She entered the restaurant and saw Matisse wave her over from a far corner near the bar. Smiling at the hostess, Emily walked to the table and sat down opposite him. The server was quick, and Emily ordered a Caesar and a Monte Cristo.

"I'm really glad you decided to come," Matisse started as he sipped his Caesar. "I wasn't sure you'd actually show up."

Emily gave Matisse a leveled stare. "What do you want, Matisse?"

"I don't want anything, Emily." Shocked, Matisse sat back. "I've missed your company since you've been gone."

"It's only been about four months. We were all just away together, remember?" Emily asked as the server arrived with her drink.

"I know, but we don't really talk in-between those family get-togethers."

"It sounds like you guys see quite a bit of Conrad still?"

"He comes by when he has the kids or for a drink when he's back from work. Why?"

"Just wondering. Seems like he's been hanging around you guys a lot."

"He's our friend, too, you know. Just because you broke it off with him doesn't mean that everyone you both knew was going to stop hanging out with him."

Emily's face became flush with anger. *I didn't expect that, but some loyalty would have been nice.* She excused herself and went to the bathroom. She dabbed at her eyes in the mirror as angry tears threatened to ruin her fake confidence. She took a couple of deep breaths. *What the hell am I doing?*

Emily's food was on the table when she got back, and Matisse had already started eating.

"Don't you miss us at all?" he said between mouthfuls.

Emily stopped midbite, "I never miss *us*, because there never was an *us*. I told you the last time we had this conversation?"

"I'm going to be down here a lot more on business. I thought maybe you'd like some familiar company."

"I don't need any familiar company," she said. Emily put her fork down and placed her hands in her lap, sitting up and staring Matisse straight. "Matisse ... you don't think there's still something here, do you? Between us?"

She watched Matisse's face as his eyes scanned her. Flashes of emotion ran through them. "We've already been through this. It's like *déjà vu*, Matisse.

Matisse took another bite of his sandwich while staring down at his plate, head hung, and shoulders slumped. He swallowed, took another bite, and looked up at Emily, his brown eyes filled with longing. "There could have been ..."

"You know what ... I think it was a mistake meeting you for lunch. I thought we could catch up on our lives over the last few months, not rehash old history."

Emily picked up her purse and put her coat on. Taking some cash from her wallet, she set it on the table. "I'm not interested in pursuing this, Matisse. I'm not interested in talking about it anymore, either. I suggest you do your best to concentrate on making your life with Anika better." With that, Emily left the restaurant.

CHAPTER 12

Slowing her pace as the treadmill timer announced the end, Emily pulled the earbuds out her phone and stepped off, steadying herself before walking toward the locker room. She turned the shower on and listened to a voicemail from Andrea as she organized her needed toiletries.

"Hey Emily. Not sure what you're up to this weekend, but Susan … we met her at the park, she has four kids under six" Andrea sounded excited and rushed as she babbled through the message. "Anyway, she's having a passion party at her house this weekend – actually, tonight. I'm hoping you can make it. Let me know if you have the girls as I have a babysitter coming to coming to watch Mackenzie. We shouldn't be too late. Call me back,"

Emily smiled, pulled off her sweaty garments and relished the warm shower in the coolness changing area room.

***

Emily called Andrea once she was in the car and on the way home. She loved the friendship they had formed in the year since Emily had moved. Andrea had helped make Vancouver feel like the home.

She considered her options for the evening and weekend while waiting for Andrea to pick up.

Hey, Emily! You got my message," Andrea answered, out of breath. "Do I need to let the babysitter know to expect two more?"

"I don't have the kids this weekend, actually. Conrad picked them up from school yesterday and has them until Sunday afternoon."

"Oh, Great! We can have a few drinks then and you can stay at my place if you want."

"Maybe," Emily replied, debating whether she wanted to forfeit a night alone in her own bed for staying up late and visiting with Andrea and her friends, "Drinks for sure! I can always take a cab home late or something."

"Sounds great. We can walk to Susan's from my place. Meet me here at seven?"

"See you then." While she concentrated on driving home, Emily also let her thoughts wander. She didn't know Susan very well, but they all seemed to get along great when they'd met at the park last summer. After that, Emily had stuck to herself a lot while she kept busy with work and the girls.

But if she had to be honest with herself, there were parts of her old life she missed, mostly Anika. She felt naked with her new freedom and still endured guilt when she did have fun without her. It was a delicate balance between finding out who she was, who she had been and who she was going to be.

Emily sighed and shook her head to rid herself of nagging memories that threatened to take away the evening's excitement. Back at the apartment she felt loud music and a glass of honey jack on ice was in. She danced around the house in her pink and purple polka-dot underwear as she finished her first glass and filled it again, making the conscious decision to take a cab to Andrea's.

Slipping slowly out of her underwear in front of the large bathroom mirror, Emily studied her body. She had started back at the gym just after Christmas. She was on her way to 40, but she looked younger. *Good genes,* she thought to herself as she looked at the ever so evident lines on her face.

Allowing her eyes to fall lower, she gauged her breasts: still even, despite two children and weight gains and losses. Her stomach and hips held stretch marks from growing too quickly as a teenager and as a mother. The white and opaque lines used to bother her, but she felt proud of them now.

She was raising two beautiful, challenging, wonderfully complex daughters; children she had brought into the world. There was no shame to be had in that at all. Emily rested her eyes on her unshaven self. There had been no reason as of late to shave, save for the occasional trip to the public pool with the kids and for her own comfort.

Emily swallowed the last of the alcohol and wrinkled up her forehead. Placing the cup on the marble counter, she ran her hand over her breasts and down past her belly button. She watched her face as she made slow circles lower and lower. It had been too long since she had pleasured herself. She often forgot how much stress it relieved for her.

Biting her bottom lip, she rhythmically ran her fingers around her clit in circles to send a shiver of warmth through the muscles of her vagina. Bringing her other hand to her breast, Emily gently squeezed her nipple, pulling it away from her, and she let out a cry.

She increased her speed down below and the hand on her breast met pace until she let out her release, loud and raw. Leaning forward, she caught herself on the counter and panted as the contractions of her orgasm subsided.

Looking toward the mirror again, she saw her flushed face, her blue eyes wide and shining with pleasure. Biting her bottom lip once again, she smiled at herself then turned in search of an outfit for the night.

***

Two hours later, Emily and Andrea were walking toward Susan's. Three blocks later the two rang the bell. Hearing the laughter inside they smiled at each other. Then they opened the door having heard, "Come in!" from somewhere amid the laughter.

"Hey!" Emily called out as she peeked her head around the corner into the living room. There were seven other women sitting on various pieces of furniture. An older woman, in her fifties, unpacked a large sample case and put the items on display. Emily blushed as she realized it was a collection of adult toys.

Making her way further into the room as Andrea said her hellos, Emily could see dildos and vibrators of every size, butt plugs, fuzzy hand cuffs and an assortment of lubes and creams. It had been many years since she had explored this avenue of sex, and she felt her face become hot and flushed, but she also felt a warmth spread down to between her legs.

"Emily!" Andrea called, waving an arm to bring her over to the kitchen where she and Susan stood, "Do you want a glass of wine?"

"That would be great. Red, if you have it." Emily smiled and embraced Susan as Andrea removed a wine glass from the cupboard and poured a glass of cab sav for Emily. "How are you, Susan? Thanks so much for the invite tonight!"

"I'm glad you could make it. Who did you find to babysit?"

"The girls' dad has the kids for the weekend, so the timing worked out perfect." Emily took the glass of wine from Andrea and gave Susan a tight smile. Just the mention of Conrad made her uncomfortable, and it worried her enough to know she had no control over what he was doing with them without having to talk about it.

"Well, tonight is going to be full of laughs and fun. Something I think you need!" Susan winked and strode to the fridge. Returning to the living room with a tray of jello shots, she let out a loud whistle to get everyone's attention. "Hello, ladies! Now that we're all here, just a couple of housekeeping bits. The washroom is down the hall to the left, there's wine in the kitchen, both red and white. Appys are on the table.

"We're all here to have fun, have a few giggles and best of all learn about and take home some new tricks to help melt away our stress, if you know what I mean!" Susan smiled widely and elbowed Emily in the ribs as she spoke the last part. Emily took another large gulp of her wine and smiled. "Now, over to Lidia to give us the ins and outs, no pun intended," Susan laughed at her own joke, "of the latest and greatest ways to pleasure ourselves and our partners."

Lidia grinned, thanked Susan, then got right down to business, "Women's pleasure has taken a backseat for far too long. There are countless health benefits to the female orgasm, but women aren't reaping them. It could be we aren't feeling connected with our partners, or maybe we're too tired at the end of the day, or it might just plain well be we've forgotten to make ourselves, and our sexual health, a priority. Who can relate?"

Everyone in the room shot their hands up and laughed in embarrassment.

"It's time women in their thirties, forties and beyond start taking back what belongs to us! Now, I have a few questions. I will just ask you to raise your hand, but don't feel pressured to answer if you're uncomfortable. Okay?"

"Sounds great to me!" Susan said loudly, walking around the room with the shots, "I think a couple of jello shots will get everyone loosened up enough to forget about being embarrassed."

"So, by a show of hands, how many of you have sex or masturbate on a weekly basis?" No one raised their hands. "Really? Come on … don't be shy."

Two women on a loveseat across the room put their hands up and giggled. Taking their shots and downing them quickly, they looked back at Lidia, giggling like teenagers.

Emily looked closer. They seemed familiar but couldn't place where they were from.

"That's great! And there is absolutely no reason to be embarrassed. Women who orgasm on a regular basis tend to sleep and deal with stress better. Plus, there's the added benefit of the glow that comes afterwards." Lidia turned to her display and pointed at the various items she had lain out. "Enough of me talking for a bit! I'm going to pass around some of the item's I've brought. Let me know if you have any questions about any of them or if you're ready to make a purchase."

The women started talking quietly amongst each other and giggling as Lidia passed around a mix of the sex toys for everyone to look over and discuss. Standing in front of Emily, Lidia handed her a bright pink, curved, double-ended dildo. She blushed and took it from the woman, who gave her a big smile and walked away.

Emily turned it over in her hands, the silkiness of the shaft and the girth made her lower regions start to ache with the need for release once again. She closed her eyes for a moment and could almost smell Anika on her, in her. Her smooth skin next to her own, fingers sliding in and out.

Emily opened her eyes and looked around, her face flush. Everyone else was busy looking at the other toys, so they hadn't even noticed Emily's absence for the moment.

Shaking her head to dispel the leftover thoughts of the passion that had reignited her enjoyment for sex, Emily finished her wine in one quick gulp and decided to really get down to business with these toys. She was a grown woman, after all, and single at that. A woman had needs, and she intended to purchase enough to satisfy her own, and perhaps something to satisfy a future partner's needs as well.

She stood at the table and picked up a glass butt plug. It was smooth and weighted. Emily made a mental note to include one of those. Turning to Lidia she asked, "May I have an order sheet and catalogue?"

"Yes! Do you have any questions about how any of the products work?"

"I don't think so."

"Let me know if you do. Oh! And if you spend over $150 you get free lube and cleaner!"

"Great! Thanks!" Emily found a comfortable spot on the floor, pen, order sheet, and catalogue in hand. She flipped through the vibrators first. The choices were endless: double ended, double penetration, clit stimulators. Emily chose two of the vibrators and a double ended dildo. Deciding on a butt plug with a purple and pink-marbled design on it, she flipped to the fetish section. She felt her face flush as she looked at whips, riding crops and handcuffs.

I'm not sure I'm quite there yet.

Doing a quick tally, she realized she was $10 short of the freebies. Going back through the catalogue, Emily decided on a set of vibrating nipple clamps. "You never know," she said under her breath, smiling and shrugging her shoulders as she filled out the rest of the shipping and payment information. Handing her order to Lidia, but keeping the catalogue, she turned in search of Andrea, and more wine.

"Did you find anything good?" Susan asked as she intercepted Emily. She giggled, her face flushed with wine, and gave Emily a one-armed hug. "You single girls need to have something to keep you satisfied."

Susan was still married to her high school sweetheart, and, despite the usual arguments about missed hampers and dish duty, even four kids later they had a pretty decent marriage. *At least on the outside because you never know what goes on behind closed doors.* She scowled at her own negativity and returned Susan's hug. Emily smiled and winked.

Andrea came down the hallway and smiled when she noticed Susan's arm around Emily. In turn, Emily shrugged and grinned in response.

Once Susan flitted off to visit with some of the other ladies, she asked Emily, "Did you buy anything?"

"A few things. How about you?"

"Nah, I bought the last time Susan had one of these. Nothing new to add to my tickle trunk right now."

"Should we get going?" Emily asked as their giggles subsided and they both finished their wine.

"Sure."

Emily crossed the room, lost in her thoughts as she picked her way across the busy carpet filled with order forms, catalogues, sex toys and women. Stumbling over an outstretched leg, Emily went to mumble sorry when the person connected to the leg looked at her.

"Emily?" the woman asked as she moved her leg and met Emily's eyes. Emily's face flushed, then paled.

"Yes. Sorry. I can be such a klutz. Are you okay?"

"Yeah. Your Emily Eckhart? Right?"

"Yes, why?" Emily felt her stomach start to do flips as she still couldn't place the woman in front of her. "Do I know you?"

"Kind of … I know some of the same people you do. I'm Becka. I know your husband, Conrad."

"He's not my husband," Emily snapped. She immediately regretted her outburst and made a move toward the door in hopes of a quicker exit.

VANESSA M. THIBEAULT

"Oh, right," Becka replied, looking at the woman she was sitting with, then laughing.

"Is something funny?" Emily asked. She stood straighter as she looked down at Becka, still sitting relaxed on the floor, leaning back on her hands.

"No. Well ..." she scoffed, looking at her friend again, smirking. "I heard you left him for another woman and cheated on him before that. Must be tough to have such a hard-working man and not know how to keep him."

"Pardon me?" Emily reddened and she took a deep breath.

Becka looked at Emily and laughed again. Then, she leaned forward and took another jello shot as she kept eye contact with Emily. "You heard me."

"I don't know what you've heard, but I can tell you right now – if it came out of Conrad's mouth, it's a load of crap. He's a liar and was a terrible husband. Also, quite frankly, it's none of your fucking business."

Andrea came around the corner as the rest of the room quieted down to watch the scene unfold. She looked from Emily to Becka and back again. "You okay, Em?"

Emily stood staring at Becka and ignored Andrea as she watched the younger woman stand and straighten her shirt and jeans. Emily crossed her arms over her chest and breathed deeply, holding back the anger that threatened to come out. Becka's smug look angered her further.

"At least he wasn't the one who cheated," Becka said.

"You have no idea what you're talking about."

"Em," Andrea reached and touched Emily's shoulder. "Let's go, okay?"

Emily put her shoes on and was out the door before she even had her jacket on. Angrily marching away from Susan's house, she tried to get her jacket on while not dropping her purse. Andrea caught up and held her jacket while Emily found the armhole and zipped it up against the cold.

Andrea kept pace with Emily for a block before Emily spoke, "What a fucking bitch!" she yelled, her face to the sky.

"I'm sorry, Emily. I didn't know you knew Becka."

"I don't, but apparently my piece of shit ex-husband does."

They walked in silence, Emily finally slowing her pace, allowing them both to catch their breath. "Do you want to come in for a drink before you go home?" Andrea asked

"No thanks. I'm just going to call a cab and go home."

"I'd probably do the same."

***

"Hey, Conrad. It's just me, Emily. Your EX-WIFE. I just met a friend of yours, Becka …"

Emily trailed off and let silence fall on the voicemail for a moment, "She had some interesting things to tell me that you'd said about me. I'd sure like to talk about them. Give me a call."

Emily hung up and resisted the urge to throw her phone across the room. She was still boiling after the confrontation with Becka and, after leaving Andrea's and returning to her apartment, she had continued to drink.

"I can't believe the nerve of him," she talked out loud to herself as she lay on the floor in her living room and sipped honey jack from a straw without having to sit up. "What a fucking cunt!"

She picked up her phone and decided to call Anika. No answer there either, so Emily decided to leave another voicemail, "Hey Anika … I'm not sure what is going on, but some bitch down this way, who knows Conrad apparently, says that he said that she knows I cheated on him and left him for a woman …. I am not sure who was blabbing bullshit or who started rumors, but I really need an ear right now. Call me if you can."

Emily finished her drink and stumbled her way to the

bathroom to run a bath. Water always made her happy. She sat on the edge of the tub, carefully taking off her socks and then steadying herself to take off the rest of her clothes so as not to fall over. Just as she was removing her blouse, her cell sounded with a text message. It was Anika.

Sorry I missed your call. We were just playing a game.

Emily paused as she read the text. Her stomach lurched as her intuition tingled with what was just out of reach of her. The same nagging feeling that had been at her all evening.

No worries. Who all is over?

Emily waited for a response as she got into the tub. Ten minutes passed, and she started to become agitated. Anika's text was abrupt and impersonal. Furling her brow, she sunk under the water and blew out all her air. She stayed under for as long as she could, then popped her head up and gasped for air. She noticed that her phone was flashing with a text.

Conrad and the girls are here.

Emily read and reread the text. Confusion set in first, then anger. *She told me our friendship was more important. She told me she disliked him just as much as I did and that she supported me. Now she's voluntarily hanging out with him and my kids.* Emily's internal dialogue started to feel shaky and jealous.

Oh? Emily texted back.

She didn't really expect a response this time from her text. And, if she were honest with herself, didn't want one. Emily drained the tub and brushed her teeth. Leaving her hair unbrushed, she slathered lotion on her face and crawled into bed.

Her skin was sensitive from the hot bath and the anger coursing through her. The soft flannel sheets felt comforting and welcoming as she fell into her feather pillow and took a few deep breaths. Willing the hot tears to go away was useless. She rolled over and let them come. Sobs rocked her to sleep as she allowed the emptiness to swallow her.

CHAPTER 13

Emily pulled into the Walmart parking lot searching for Conrad's truck. Emily had driven the girls up to Conrad on Friday and he was now returning them to her. It was a little more than a four-hour round trip, but they each needed to do their part.

As she turned down a mostly empty row, she could see Conrad's truck and the girls in the back seat. Julia was looking out the window, a sad, almost painful expression on her young face as her chin rested on the door. Emily parked a couple of spots down and Julia smiled as she noticed. Emily looked in her direction and smiled back.

Conrad hadn't noticed her arrive and turned around to say something to Claire. She made a face at Conrad and crossed her arms in defiance. As Emily got closer, she could hear Claire's yells of frustration.

Looking inside, Emily saw Conrad laughing and smiling while Claire cried and yelled some more. When she opened Claire's door, Conrad was still grinning. Emily stared at him in disbelief and pulled Claire out. Julia scrambled toward her as well and launched herself into her mother's arms. "I missed you, Mommy," Julia stated with a smile.

"I missed you too, sweetie," Emily kissed Julia and put her on the ground. Taking her hand, she walked the younger sister to the car. "You wait here while I get Claire, okay?"

Julia nodded her agreement and scampered into the back seat of the SUV. Emily turned around to see Claire still upset and Conrad staring at her, a half smile on his face, leaning against his truck.

Emily's heart beat a little faster as she contemplated her choices. Conrad and Emily never had a direct physical altercation while they were married, but there had been intimidation, isolation, and bullying.

Claire stomped her feet and continued yelling as Emily watched Conrad laugh at her again. He made a face at Claire and mimicked her stomped feet. Emily reddened and felt embarrassed for Claire as she screamed, "STOP IT!"

"You can't do that, Conrad." Emily stepped around him, finally taking a stand. "She's eight, and you're a full-grown man. You only see her once a month at best and, besides that, you're supposed to teach her how to be respectful."

Conrad pointed a finger over Emily's shoulder at Claire and crossed his arms over his chest, staring down at Emily. "Not seeing the kids is your fault, Emily. And I don't have to do what she tells me to. She can't act this way."

"Stop it!" Claire yelled, stomping her foot like a toddler.

"Claire, go to the car and wait for me," Emily instructed. "Watch for other vehicles."

Claire furled her brow and crossed her arms, then uncrossed them and balled her hands into fists. Tense shoulders up at her ears, she stomped into the SUV and slammed the door. Glaring through the window she slumped down in the seat and pulled her hood on.

"Come on, Conrad! You can't think of anything better to do than antagonize your eight-year-old? Grow up!"

Conrad stared at her, arms hanging limply at his sides, a blank expression on his face. He shifted his weight around as he leaned. He shrugged his shoulders and made no move to leave or respond.

"What was the issue?" Emily asked, looking for clarification on what had ensued before she had intervened. As much as she hated Conrad, she still expected more from her daughters. Despite his poor example and emotionally abusive tendencies, she was going to raise kind, strong, respectful women. If a consequence was needed for disrespectful behaviour, then Emily would, although reluctantly and painfully, follow through on consistent consequences. Conrad was making his own bed with his daughters by treating them the way he did.

"I told her to quit singing while Julia and I were talking, and she didn't listen. She kept getting louder, so I told her she was grounded for two weeks and she freaked out like she always does."

"Did you try talking to her? Try making sure she knew you weren't excluding her, but wanted to hear her, too?"

"I don't have to explain myself to her. She needs to just listen."

Emily gritted her teeth and found herself clenching her fists in the pocket of her coat. Taking a deep breath, she closed her eyes and tried to speak in calm tones, "I will not be following through on the two weeks of grounding. You're not here and, quite frankly, that's an over the top punishment for her actions-"

"Yeah, why not just let them know what I say doesn't matter, hey? You just do whatever you want anyways. Breaking up our family. You're fucking those kids up, you know?" Conrad spoke in a calm tone, but with disgust in his voice. Guilt-laden words cut Emily as they were spat at her.

"I didn't break our family up. You did when you quit respecting me." Emily walked away, resisting the urge to finger Conrad as she walked away. Stopping at her car, she took two steps back toward him. "Who's Becka, Conrad?"

Confusion came over Conrad's face, then recognition of the name Emily had just spoken, "Uh ... who?" He stuttered and ran a hand through his hair.

"Becka. She said she knows you. There were some interesting things she informed me you'd said."

Conrad shrugged and leaned back against his truck. "I think she's one of my buddy's sisters."

"We'll have this conversation another time. Make sure you get your story straight, Conrad." She got into her car and started the engine.

"I love you, Mom," Claire said quietly from the backseat. Dried tears on her face. She didn't look angry anymore, just sad and defeated.

"I love you, Claire. I love you too, Julia."

"Love you, Mommy!" Julia chirped.

"Are your seatbelts on?" Emily asked putting hers on as well. Turning around to double check they were safe, Emily asked, "What song do you girls want to listen to?"

Conrad was still standing against his truck staring at Emily as she pulled out of the lot. Giving him a hard stare, she drove past, singing loudly with her girls. Music always helped them process their emotions, and when they listened to it together, it was like therapy. They could release and express themselves.

***

At home, Emily started the girls a warm bubble bath and let them play for close to an hour. They looked like prunes when they finally emerged in fluffy purple towels and then their favorite pajamas. Emily had prepared an easy meal of miso soup, peppers and grilled cheese, and they sat together on the floor in the living room and watched a feel-good movie.

They all needed a break from the day. The time together, without expectation, felt wonderful for all of them.

As Emily tucked Claire into bed, her daughter's small arms tightly wound around her. "I don't want to go with Dad next time."

Emily froze. What was she supposed to say? She didn't want to force a relationship that was obviously damaging and hurtful, but Conrad was still her father, and Emily didn't have any real grounds to refuse him access. On top of that, there was no way she was going to allow Julia to go with Conrad by herself. The girls needed to stay together, stick together.

"Sweetie, I think you had a long day and not much sleep this weekend. I want us to talk about this more in the morning. I know you're hurt and upset. You need to make sure you're being respectful as well, right?"

"I know, Mom. I still don't want to go again."

"Okay, Claire," Emily replied, hugging her daughter again and giving her a firm kiss on the cheek, "I promise we will talk about this more, okay?"

"Okay."

"Good night." Turning to Julia's bed, she was snuggled up holding a stuffed cat in her arms. "Good night, Julia."

"Good night, Mommy. I don't want to go with daddy if Claire's not going."

"We will talk about this when we are all rested, okay?" Emily gave Julia a hug and kissed her cheek as well.

"Okay," Julia replied, "Can you kiss Missus Meow, too, please?"

Emily laughed and gave the stuffed cat a big kiss and a tucked the blankets around Julia. Tucking the blankets around Claire on more time, she retreated, leaving the door open a crack.

CHAPTER 14

Emily had just sat down, book in hand and tea on the coffee table, when her phone vibrated. Looking at the caller ID she saw it was Anika. Emily flushed as the anger from last night and this afternoon filled her. She sent the call to voicemail and sat on the couch staring at the wall, her book on her lap.

"Why..." she muttered. She fell face first into the couch and yelled into the cushions. Anika always seemed to be playing a side. Even when they were together, Anika would say she was on Emily's side with things, but she was constantly standing up for Conrad or his actions.

Emily's phone rang again, and she decided not to ignore it this time. "Hello?" she asked into it, her voice calm while she balled her fists up in the blanket beside her.

"Hey. How are you? I'm sorry I couldn't talk the other night."

"Yeah. That's okay. You had company, right?" Emily was curt and didn't bother to ask Anika how their evening was with Conrad and the girls.

"Yeah," Anika paused. Emily could hear the faint sound of water running in the background.

"Do you know a Becka?"

"Hmm. Yeah, I think I do. I think you do, too. Isn't that Liam's little sister, from the post office? The one who transferred down to where you are?"

"That kind of rings a bell. Does Conrad know her?" Emily tried to piece together the names she knew, but she had never been very good at keeping track of who was who in any circle.

"Conrad knows that whole group…" Anika trailed off and coughed. Emily waited for her to continue, but she didn't offer any more.

"How does he know the whole group?" Emily asked, her curiosity piqued at Anika's less than forthcoming comment. "Who else is in the group, Anika? I kind of need to know. I'm tired of running into people who know me, or think they know me, who I have no idea about."

"Becka is Liam's little sister. Liam is married to Charlene who is childhood friends with Clint. Clint and Conrad go shooting together. They work up at the same place, same shifts. They all get together when they're back from work on the weekends that Conrad doesn't have the kids," Anika hesitated as she answered. Emily felt like she was holding back something.

"That still doesn't explain how Becka would have any idea I cheated on Conrad. He doesn't even know I slept with you and Matisse."

"Emily, Anika began quietly, clearing her throat. "Matisse may have let it slip that you and I were together a few times."

"What the hell?" Emily yelled and stood abruptly. "How the hell does that come up in everyday conversation? What did you say?"

"I wasn't there. Matisse and Conrad were out with Liam, Mike and Clint and they'd been drinking. They were talking about women, and Matisse says he slipped up, and said he'd seen me with another woman … Conrad's the one that guessed it. Matisse just didn't deny it."

"What did you say to Matisse when he told you?"

"I was livid, obviously! I told him it was supposed to be something between just us. It wasn't for advertising."

"Anika, do you know what the backlash on this could be?"

"Don't think I don't know, but you won't be the only one hurting if this gets out anymore. My reputation is on the line as well. You just happened to have the option to get up and leave. I have to face everyone where I am. Everyone who knows everyone who know me."

"I didn't just decide to up and leave, Anika. You know that. You can't just say I left like that. It wasn't that simple." Tears streamed down Emily's face, and she shook as the ramifications sunk in. Emily hadn't come out to anyone, and now, being separated from Conrad, not dating, and these rumours floating around, something was sure to come back. She just hoped there wouldn't be any backlash on the girls.

"You know what, Emily? There are always other options. You decided to choose the one you did, and you need to live with it. Just the same as you would have had to live with a decision to stay. Shit happens, and we are all at risk for Matisse's stupidity, but we can't go back and change it. It is what it is." Anika fell silent, though the hurt in her voice was evident.

"Why didn't you tell me about Matisse?"

Silence filled the line for several minutes. Neither woman spoke. Emily waffled between being bitterly angry and tearfully hurt.

"I have to go, Emily."

"Anika —" Emily tried, but Anika had already hung up.

She stared at the phone, at Anika's name in her contacts. She gently set it down on the table, then watched the screen dim to blackness.

She thinks I left her. She honestly believes that, Emily thought as her tears dried.

CHAPTER 15

Emily answered the phone out of breath as she slammed the apartment door behind her. "Hello?" She didn't have a chance to look at the caller ID before answering.

"Ms. Eckhart?"

"Speaking."

"This is David Hawes, vice principal at the school. I have Claire here in the office with me."

"Oh, no. What happened?" Emily stopped putting groceries away and sat down at the bar, her head in her hand as she listened.

"Well, we would like you to come down. Claire got in a fight today."

"Oh, jeez. Okay. I'll be there shortly. Can you take Julia out of class, so she doesn't take the bus, please?"

"We will make sure she's here when you arrive."

"Crap!" Emily cursed as she hung up the phone. Grabbing her keys and purse from the floor where she had flung them, Emily rushed back out to her car. Thirty minutes later, she was in the school's office, unsure what she was walking into.

Claire waited on a chair next to Julia beside vice principal's office. Julia got up and hugged her mom. Emily squeezed her body close to hers.

Claire looked up and met Emily's eyes, then slumped back in her chair. Her brow was furled, and her arms were crossed tightly over her chest as she kicked her backpack. Her nose had the remnants of blood, but other than that, she looked unscathed. There were no other children in the office, though the hallways bustled with afterschool activity.

"Hi, Ms. Eckhart?" Mr. Hawes asked.

"Emily, please."

"Emily. In here, please," Mr. Hawes indicated, as he stepped toward his office. "Claire, you stay out here for now, please."

Claire neither responded nor looked at the vice principal while she continued to kick her backpack.

Emily knelt down next to her daughter, "Claire. You need to respond to Mr. Hawes," she said firmly.

"Yes, Mr. Hawes," Claire reluctantly replied through mumbled lips.

Emily sighed and glared at her daughter as she followed the vice principal into his office. She sat on the edge of the available chair. "What happened?"

"Well, Claire got into a fight today. From what I can piece together from her, the other student, and the supervisors, she was making fun of her classmates while on the monkey bars. When one of the kids fell, Claire went up and laughed in her face as she tried to get up. The other student pushed Claire, and she pushed back, knocking her down. Claire kicked her, and the other student hit her in the nose as a playground monitor arrived to break it up."

"Where's the other student?"

"Her dad already picked her up. She's been asked to stay home for the remainder of the week. Emily, how are things at home?"

"Umm …" Emily was caught off guard. She thought she was doing a good job with the girls, but there obviously seemed to be a disconnect between what she did and what Claire took school as acceptable behaviour. "I think things have been alright. We've had a lot of changes over the last year, but I thought she had adjusted well. There haven't been any huge issues."

"How is Claire's relationship with her dad? I know you two are divorced –"

"Things are strained there. He doesn't really see the kids, and when he does … well, it is less than ideal."

"I think some of her issues stem from that situation. We have access to wonderful resources here at school and throughout the community. Books, pamphlets, counselors, those sorts of things."

"Thank you, Mr. Hawes –"

"David, please."

"David, thank you, but for now I think we're alright. I still have the number of the social worker the school contacted back in the fall. Do you have a number or website I can go to if I change my mind for other resources??"

"Of course." David handed her a card and a booklet. "I think Claire should stay home tomorrow. Maybe have a talk with her and spend some time trying to figure out what's going on. We're going to do up a school action plan and go over it with her and the other student on Monday for their behaviour."

"Thank you," Emily said, as she rose to leave.

"On a personal note, I know how hard divorce can be on children. If you ever need someone to talk to, I know first-hand what it's like trying to raise kids on your own."

Emily looked at the vice-principal as she placed the card and booklet in her purse. She forced a smile.

"Thank you, Mr. Hawes," she said, then exited the office with Claire in hand. She located Julia waiting for her outside and the three of them got into the car.

Both girls were silent as Emily navigated home during the start of rush hour traffic.

***

"I don't have my head in the sand," Anika told Emily. "I know who my kids are. I know what they need work on. But I think ... the boys don't fit into that category. They've got their stuff, but they're not the ones with the behavioural issues like you see from the other kids," she spat with disdain, disgust and some sort of sympathy. "It's the other kids that provoke them into the way the are. Not the other way around. They need that rigid classroom to keep all the kids in check."

Emily nodded. What was she supposed to say from this far away? She didn't have any direct contact with the twins since moving, but she knew what a handful they had been. Emily knew there were going to be challenges along the way but was always made to feel that what she had to say didn't matter.

I'm tired of her thinking that they're not the issue. Emily thought as she slammed dishes away in her cupboards. She was tired of being made the fool, tired of being made to believe that the way she thought meant nothing. It wasn't the way she was that was the issue, it wasn't the way her kids were that were the issue. It wasn't even the way the past seemed to repeat itself with Emily that was the issue. Emily did all she could to make her home better. She did all she could to make the lives she touched better.

"I'm worried about report cards. I'm worried what their teacher is going to have to say. I'm not going to be nice. I'm going to go in there with my hair raised and want the best for my kids."

"I know, Anika," Emily started. "You're a great mom, and I think you should go in there with their best interests at heart. I think you need to ask what is being done to support the kids that don't fit into the lower end of the classroom and what is being done to support the higher ones as well. Don't leave any of it unanswered."

"I don't think they're being given a fair chance to do good in the class …" Anika paused. Emily could hear her taking a drink. Emily cringed at the use of the word 'good' but didn't correct Anika.

"I know you feel you need some more answers about what is going on in the classroom," Emily said.

"What do you mean by that?" Anika sounded agitated and annoyed. Emily knew she had been hoping to have a clear supporter; someone who would have agreed with all her points about her sons, but Emily wasn't about to do that. She didn't believe that, nor did she believe that all the issues with the boys had to do with a lack of classroom control. She had seen how the boys could behave; how they could manipulate and escalate situations and then make it seem like it was someone else's fault.

"Nothing is meant by it at all. I'm sorry there's so much stress around the kids' school."

"I know you don't agree with me."

"Anika, I didn't say that."

"You don't have to. It's fine. It's just not something you would understand."

"Anika," Emily replied exasperated.

"What else is new with you?" Anika changed the subject. Emily could hear the frustration and annoyance in her voice and decided not to push the issue any further, "How are Claire and Julia?"

"They're doing well. It's been a bit of a challenge with Claire and school as of late, but she seems to have overcome the obstacles of being the new kid."

"Oh?" Anika asked quizzically. Heavy silence lingered between them. "What happened?"

"Claire got into a fight at school. There was some shoving and some disrespect being given out."

"That sounds like Claire," Anika snickered.

"What do you mean by that?" Emily felt her face start to heat and her defences go up. She gripped the phone tighter.

"Well, she's always had trouble keeping her mouth shut. Guess she had to learn the hard way."

"It wasn't exactly like that, Anika. And there have been a few things with Conrad which Claire's behaviour happens to be mimicking."

"Okay, Emily," Anika replied curtly.

"Okay, Anika," Emily replied with the same venom. She immediately regretted sinking to the level of being sarcastic. She had no intention of hurting Anika. Frustrated, Emily sat down heavily on the edge of her couch, "I'm sorry, Anika."

Anika didn't immediately reply. The sound of cleanup was replaced by silence between the two women. "Anika?" Emily inquired, sighing.

"Still here," she replied, not offering an apology of her own.

Their conversation faded to small talk about work, school, and less serious topics about the kids. It had been close to a month since they had talked, and, although Emily had a lot she had wanted to tell Anika, she hesitated to share her news about Izzy and her new friends.

She didn't want to hurt her. Plus, she didn't want to have to deal with issues that were going to ensue when she finally realized that she wasn't hanging on to the unrealistic dream that Anika was at some point going to leave Matisse and they would finally find themselves together.

A few minutes later, Emily hung up the phone and peeked in at the girls in their room. She found them sitting on Claire's bed reading books together. Watching for a few minutes, she saw Claire stop what she was doing to help Julia with the word she struggled with. *At least it looks like I'm doing something right,* she said to herself.

CHAPTER 16

Emily let her head drop to the table as her computer froze for the fourth time in an hour. Banging it against the dark wood a couple of times, she sat up and ran her hands through her blonde hair.

Maybe this is a sign I need to do something else for a bit.

Holding down the power button on her computer, she shut the screen and stacked the notebooks scattered on the kitchen table.

She went to the kitchen and opened the fridge. She wanted something easy and comforting to eat, but she'd been trying to have less processed food in the house and feed herself better. When she was alone during the day or quietly keeping to herself in the evening it was a lot more difficult to convince herself not to eat the ice cream, leftover Halloween candy, or the nachos and cheese sauce that called to her from the cupboards.

Today felt different, though. She opened each cupboard and moved things around. Next, she opened the silverware drawer and began to reorganize and place the forks and knives in order; kids helping to put things away often meant they weren't done so in the neatest of ways.

Emily stopped and took a breath. Realizing she was feeling restless and heavy, she needed to figure out where this feeling came from. She decided to have a bath.

Bringing a cup of tea with her, she sat in the tub while it filled. Watching the water slowly cover her feet, ankles, then legs, she rested her chin on her knees. Breathing deep she took a sharp breath in as she realized what may be making her so anxious: *Conrad,* she thought to herself, *he hasn't emailed or texted me back about his visitation.*

Emily picked up the phone and sent him another text after checking her email. The joint custody they had agreed on seemed to be working. Depending on where the girls were with their schoolwork and holidays, Conrad came down once a month to pick them up for anywhere between three to five days. Sometimes he stayed in the area at a hotel or a friend's house. Other times, he drove them back to their original house.

When Emily and the girls had first moved, Conrad put up some resistance with the schedule she insisted upon. Yet, he didn't miss a visit over the past six months. There was always previous communication about pick up and drop off ever since he had taken the girls from school to the aquarium without telling her.

Emily still had hesitations with him. Even when they were together, his parenting hadn't always been the best, and taking their needs into consideration wasn't something he did very well. Emily wanted the least amount of conflict and stress for the girls, and if she was being honest, for herself.

She had suggested he book his time off to accommodate taking the girls for extended periods of time. He was the one who didn't want to move with her. After all, why shouldn't he be the one to travel? It's not like he was home much before.

A stress-free setup was the only reason she had fought with Conrad for this type of visitation. He made some noise about having to travel to see them, but she made the argument that he had the time. Although her schedule was flexible, she couldn't take days off in the middle of the week to drive the girls to and from their old place.

She didn't ask Conrad for child or spousal support. She only wanted him to make the effort, financially and timewise, to see his children. She didn't want to have to go to court to figure out custody. She felt she could be giving and reasonable enough to not incur the cost and stress of having to go through a custody battle. It wouldn't be good for her emotionally or financially, and it certainly would put an undue amount of stress on Julia and Claire as well.

Emily's phone dinged with a text message.

You'll be hearing from my lawyer, Conrad texted.

WHAT LAWYER? Emily quickly texted back.

Emily waited fifteen minutes for a response. Finally, getting out of the bath and putting comfy clothes on, she sat on the couch with her phone and resent the message. Another fifteen minutes passed without a response. She walked back to the kitchen and poured herself a glass of wine.

She took her first sip as there was a knock on her door. Opening it, she saw a man with an envelope. "Emily Eckhart?"

"Yes."

"I have some documents I need you to sign for."

Emily looked at the man, then down at the documents, then back at the man again, "That son of a bitch," she said, her face flushed. Looking at the man again, she shook her head, "Sorry, not you."

The man smiled slightly and held out the pen and clipboard to Emily. Taking it from him, her hand shook as she signed. She handed it back to the delivery man, took the envelope and shut the door.

She slowly walked back to the kitchen as she examined the manila envelope with her name and address printed on it. Not handwritten, but typed, no return address. Ripping open the envelope, she pulled out the papers.

Scanning the documents, she realized Conrad was taking her to court for custody of Claire and Julia. "That son of a bitch," she whispered again as she finished her wine and hot tears streamed down her cheeks. She searched for Conrad's reasons for wanting custody. He listed Emily as an unfit mother and an alcoholic, that she had left and taken the girls without forewarning or due reason. He claimed she talked poorly about him in front of their daughters and encouraged them to question him and be disrespectful.

She slammed the papers down on the counter and held the bottle of wine in her hand. Then, she looked at the papers and the wine. She dumped the remainder of the bottle down the sink as she cried and washed the wine glass by hand.

She texted Andrea to call her as soon as she could. Andrea had gone through a nasty custody battle with her physically abusive ex. He tried to gain custody of their daughter on the basis that Andrea was also an unfit mother.

He had dragged her through the mud, only to be proven as the abusive, terrible person that he was. Nevertheless, Mackenzie was subjected to some terrible things by her father.

The courts seemed in favour of giving father's their due time with their children now, sometimes without the care and attention for what the situation really was. This was probably because the courts had previously been so lopsided custody-wise in favour of mother's having their children. Now, they were trying to make amends by giving fathers the benefit of the doubt, sometimes to the harm of the children involved.

Needing to keep busy, Emily vacuumed the floors, even moving the couches and tables. Pausing at the door to the girls' room, she let the tears become heavy sobs.

She fell to her knees in their doorway and let out all her frustration and anger. She had been holding it together and making it through, but she had known it wasn't going to be over with Conrad. He agreed far too easily to her terms, and now he got it in his head that the girls were better off with him. They had never been better off with him, and neither had Emily. That's exactly why she left in the first place. They were all better out of the direct clutches of his narcissistic abuse.

Painful memories of being oppressed and put down for fifteen years made her heart physically hurt. Emily remembered him telling her she'd never be able to live without him; that she needed him and couldn't do it alone. She could still hear him tell her how silly her dreams were and him laughing at her in front of the girls when she tried to parent.

She shuddered at the countless times Conrad had pressured her into having sex, even when she clearly told him she didn't want to. Even when she had begged him to stop and she cried as he got his release. She found comfort in the locked bathroom door and scorching water then, too, just like when she was a child.

Emily shakily got up from the floor and continued what she had started. Putting the furniture back, she sat at the table and pulled out one of her notebooks. She listed the qualities that made her a fit and caring mother. It took a few minutes for her to stop thinking of all the ways she failed so far.

She had a page full of positives and tangible items that could be witnessed and proved. She provided healthy meals, she was able to financially support them, and she worked from home when needed. Another page of items listed items only Emily and her daughters could corroborate.

On the next page, she listed everything that made Conrad an unfit father who shouldn't have full custody. Items at the top of the list were verbal abuse, talking negatively about Emily to the girls and making unsafe choices when they were with him. She easily filled a page with those items.

Flipping to another page, she made a list of what she now wanted to see from Conrad. She hadn't asked for anything from him. All she wanted was for Claire and Julia to have a positive relationship with their dad, even if Emily and Conrad were no longer together. She made sure she could support them on her own, she didn't ask him to contribute to even extracurricular activities or personal needs. She certainly never asked him for spousal support.

All of that was about to change. She wanted him to schedule his visits months in advance. She wanted him to pay for their extracurricular activities and at least half of what they needed, such as clothing, books, toys, school supplies, etc. She wanted a no-contact order and a court appointed officer to do the exchange between herself and Conrad.

She was done playing a part in the game he insisted on playing. She was done being manipulated and needed to be as contact-free from him as possible. There was not going to be a reconciliation. Any piece of hope that she lived with that he might change was completely gone.

Emily took out the affidavit and read it through again. She realized Conrad was looking to give her nearly the same visitation and custody that he currently had: one weekend a month, with travel being up to her, and alternating holidays and birthdays. He also included that she needed to provide him with child support since she made just as much as he did, but he would have the kids full time.

Further, Conrad requested that she pay costs for afterschool childcare and extracurricular activities. She fumed as she read his unrealistic expectations.

He doesn't even have a clue how to raise those girls.

She tossed the papers on the table and closed her eyes. She calmed her body, part by part, and tried to create a sense of peace throughout her as she formulated a plan.

She'd wait until Andrea contacted her so she could get the phone number of the lawyer she had used. Then she would make those calls and set up appointments. She would also call Anika and ask her to write a statement declaring Emily a fit mother and outline behaviours Conrad had exhibited while Emily still lived with him. Anika witnessed firsthand the putdowns and gaslighting.

Emily was worried. She had been isolated for so long with Conrad that her only real friend and confidant was Anika. What if she decided she didn't want to get involved with what was going on?

Anika had a friendship with Conrad. They got along with certain common interests and seemed to see eye-to-eye on some parenting decisions. Emily ignored the similarities and dealt with the times that they seemed more friends than her and Anika.

Emily stretched her arms high above her head. She looked at the clock and saw she still had an hour before the girls would be home. Feeling restless, she remembered that the new toys from Susan's party had arrived the day before. She had taken them out of the shipping box and placed them high in her closet, out of the prying eyes, and hands, of her curious and snoopy daughters.

Going to her room, she pulled down the box and grabbed one of the vibrators. Feeling herself rush with excitement and unreleased sexual energy, Emily unpackaged the purple appendage and slid in the batteries. It had been a long time since she used anything other than her own hand to bring herself to orgasm.

Emily slowly took her clothes off. She crawled under her feather duvet and brought the cold silicone to her warm, moist nether regions. The tool started to vibrate, and she felt herself clit quickly dampen.

Moaning out loud, Emily allowed herself to sink further into her pillows and blankets, letting her body succumb to the sensations she had foolishly been denying herself. For what reason, she didn't know. *Self-neglect, I suppose,* she thought as her mind wandered in and out of conscious thought.

Emily rubbed the vibrator over her clit and down the rest of herself. She felt the vibrating on her ass and at the opening to her vagina. Tentatively pushing it toward the opening, she felt slippery and allowed herself to relax, slipping it in effortlessly. She moaned louder as she slowly slid it in and out of herself.

Increasing her speed, Emily brought her other hand to her clit and made quick, small circles, causing her vagina to tighten in response. She cried out louder as the climax crept closer. She continued the rhythm, her hips meeting the toy in her hand, her other hand keeping pace. The cool sheets on her bed warmed as she ground herself against them in anticipation and need.

Finally, her body let go, and she screamed a needed release to the empty apartment. Her juices flowed onto her sheets as she shut off the vibrator and removed it.

She lay with her eyes closed, breathless on her back, and allowed her body to relax. She needed that. She needed an outlet, a release for the building tension. Emily smiled as her breath slowed and she felt warm beneath the blankets.

The grogginess of the orgasm slowly fading, she turned her head to look at the clock; she still had 30 minutes until the girls would be home. Picking up the vibrator, she selected a different function and sunk back into her bed once again to release the stress she held so tightly onto.

CHAPTER 17

"I just wanted the ability to be able to be kind. To let it work out on its own and have a half-decent relationship with him for the sake of the girls."

Emily sighed and stared out the window. Tucking her knees into her chest, she watched heavy snowflakes fall to the ground. It was afternoons like these that she was thankful she didn't have to drive to work.

"I'm sorry, Emily. You didn't have any idea that he would try something like this?" Andrea asked from the other end of the phone.

"Not a clue. How was I supposed to know? He'd said absolutely nothing so far and shown up for the weekends we agreed on. He didn't have any objections at all to what I suggested. I guess that should have been my first clue that he was plotting something."

"Well, the lawyer I used is your best bet. Conrad doesn't have a leg to stand on. You're none of the things he claims in the affidavit. You know that. I can vouch for you as well. What about your work or Anika? Can she help you out for the stuff from before you left? Maybe corroborate how he was when you were together?"

"I've called Anika a couple of times, but she hasn't answered. Her text messages have been short as well. I'm not really sure what's going on."

Emily let a tear slip down her cheek. She had tried to talk to Anika about what Conrad was doing but didn't get much of a response. The distance between them felt farther all the time. Emily thought she could count on Anika if things ever reached this point with Conrad, but it seemed like she was left to deal with it on her own.

It saddened Emily to realize the person who she considered to be her best friend, even after their sexual relationship needed to end with the distance between them, would dismiss her so quickly. Emily suddenly found herself very lonely. It wasn't something she sat easily with.

"Weird. I thought you guys were best friends."

"Yea, so did I." Emily looked up at the wall clock. "I should go. The girls will be coming through the door any minute. Thanks for listening, Andrea."

"Any time. Let me know what the lawyer says."

"I will. Bye."

Emily set her phone on the table and drank her tea in silence. She could hear the faint sound of traffic through the windows and the fridge running in the background. Tears dripped onto her chest as she watched the snowflakes fall lazily. She saw the school bus pull up in front of her building and stood.

Wiping her tears, Emily unlocked the apartment door and went to the kitchen to make a snack. Taking three plates out, she set cheese, crackers, celery, and apple slices out and set them on the table. Emily needed to explain to the girls about Conrad and the how their situation might be changing.

"Hi, Mom!" The girls called, slamming the door behind them. Their jackets rustled as she hung them up and brought their backpacks to the kitchen. Sitting down at the table, Emily smiled as she watched them.

"How was your day?" Emily took a bite from an apple slice and smiled at the girls.

"Oh, good," Julia replied, shoving a whole cracker in her mouth.

"Julia …" Emily scolded. Julia shrugged her shoulders and took a drink of water.

"So, girls. I have something I need to talk to you about." Emily chewed on a piece of celery and thought about how her daughters were going to react. "I talked to your dad, and he decided he wants to have someone help us figure out where you should live and how much time you will spend with each of us."

Emily paused to gauge her daughter's reactions. Julia shoved another cracker in her mouth and Claire lazily chomped on a piece of celery. "Someone, called a social worker, is going to want to talk to both of you. Your dad has told them some things about me that aren't true, and the social worker is going to ask you some questions about me your dad. I want you both to be honest and truthful. Do you understand?"

"Mom," Julia started, with her mouth full of cracker, then stopped to finish chewing and swallow after a stern look from Emily. "Why don't you and Daddy just move back in together? He could move here and see how much fun we have."

"Well …" Emily sat straighter in her chair and rested her chin on her entwined fingers, "Your dad and I don't get along sometimes. He doesn't treat me with the respect that I deserve, and I didn't think that was a fair example to set for you girls. You need to see respect and kindness."

"You yelled at dad sometimes," Claire added.

"Yes, I did. And I was wrong for that. It didn't show him the respect he deserved. But we all make mistakes. I was frustrated and felt like I was out of options."

Emily found herself becoming emotional as she tried to be strong and logical for the girls, but she still had a hard time putting her finger on the exact things that had caused her to need to move on. She shook her head as the brief thought of getting back with Conrad crossed her mind. *Never!* She thought, getting up from the table.

"There are lots of reasons why your dad and I aren't together and won't be getting back together. All I need from you both is to make sure you answer the social worker's questions in the best way you know how. Answer truthfully. Does that make sense?"

"I'm going to tell them I think you should get back together with Dad," Julia said defiantly, crossing her arms and putting her knees against the table, rocking back on her chair.

"Put your knees down at the table, Julia, and stop rocking on your chair. Your dad and I aren't getting back together."

Emily bit down on her bottom lip and took a deep breath, counting backwards from five. She was on the verge of yelling at Julia. It wasn't her fault, though. Julia didn't understand why Conrad and Emily weren't together. Julia had always pined for her father's attention, and Conrad played mind games with her just the same as he did with Emily. Pushing her away and pulling her back in. The manipulation was sickening to be a part of, let alone watch it be done to a child.

Julia continued to rock on her chair and Emily stood up from the table. Julia quickly sat up properly and spilled her water in the process. "Julia!" Emily yelled, running for a towel from the kitchen. "Enough goofing around! Just go to your room."

"Fine!" Julia yelled at her as she stomped off and slammed her bedroom door.

Emily wiped up the water and set the papers that had gotten soaked on the counter to dry. Tears of frustration and helplessness came to her eyes. She felt she had no control over the direction the next weeks were going to take. It was scary to think she might lose her girls. They were her entire life.

"I love you, Mommy," Claire chimed from where she was sat at the table. "I don't want to live with Daddy. You're happier here."

Emily broke down. She scooped Claire up into her arms. "I love you, sweetie," Emily whispered into Claire's ear. "I love you so much."

Hearing the door to Julia's bedroom open, Emily walked with Claire in her arms to the open door. Going in, she saw Julia standing with arms crossed and tears threatening to spill over her own cheeks. Emily bent down and opened her arms wide to include Julia in their hug. She reluctantly stepped forward then folded deeply into her mom and sister. They sat there on the bedroom floor until they had all quit crying.

"I love you both very much. I want the very best for you. That's all I've ever wanted. And that's why your dad and I aren't together. I will never try to keep you from him, but I don't want either of you to ever be hurt, put down, neglected, or anything ever again.

"I know most of that probably doesn't make sense to you right now, but one day it will. Whatever happens, just know I love you with all my heart, girls." Emily hugged them closer then whispered, "I think you both might need a tickle now."

With that, Emily launched her curled fingers into their ribs. Fits of giggles and squirms erupted from both.

CHAPTER 18

"How does dinner at *Lavita's* sound?" Izzy asked Emily after a few minutes of catching up from the week. They had kept in touch via phone and text over the last few weeks but didn't have the chance to meet up their talk of a few weeks prior.

Both women needed to take this slowly, especially Emily. She appreciated the control that Izzy had, especially since Emily could be very emotionally driven.

"I've never been there. What kind of food do they have?" Emily played with a twist tie left on her counter as she talked. The girls were doing their homework in their room. The warm smell of garlic, onions, and browning beef made Emily's stomach rumble. The thought of a quiet dinner with Izzy, and the possibility of what after dinner might hold, made her hunger in a different way.

"They have a small but amazing menu. Lots of seafood and local ingredients. I promise you won't be disappointed."

"That sounds great. Let me make sure I can get a babysitter before you make reservations, though, okay?"

"I'm sure Andrea can watch them," Izzy suggested.

"Uh ..." Emily stumbled and coughed on a sip of wine. "I, um ..."

"Are you okay?" Izzy asked as Emily's coughing subsided and she could catch her breath.

"Yes," Emily managed. "Izzy, I haven't exactly ... I don't think Andrea knows about us, exactly."

"I haven't said anything to her about us. I didn't think it was my place."

"It's a bit more than that." Emily's stomach did flips as she realized she hadn't exactly told Andrea, let alone anyone, about Anika or her apparent preference for women. "I haven't told Andrea that I prefer women."

There was silence on the line. Emily heard Izzy putting dishes away and waited for her to say something. Emily nervously set out dishes on the table for dinner, still waiting. "Izzy?" Emily started

"Emily, I'm as out there as it comes. I think, before we decide to pursue this any further, you need to seriously think about telling the people you are close to. If we're seen out together, I can tell you right now, word will get around."

"I wasn't trying to hide, Izzy. I ... it just hadn't come up before. It wasn't like I was actively looking for anything."

"I know, but it's not that simple. You need to tell Andrea. I know my sister, and she won't let anything change between you two. She's a great friend and has always supported my decisions. Just let me know if I should make reservations or not."

"Izzy," Emily began, then stopped. She was going to have to come to terms with being 'out' at some point. Emily had put aside her feelings about this for so long that it seemed dooming and difficult now that it was at her doorstep. "I'll call Andrea tonight and let you know if she can watch the girls."

"I know it's not easy, Emily, but if this is who you know you are, then you're going to need to tell people eventually. People will either love or hate you, and it won't matter if it's because you like pussy or not. That will just be a scapegoat they'll use."

Emily burst out laughing at the nickname for her vagina. It was one of those uncomfortable words; dirty and provocative. "Thanks for that, Izzy. Have a good night."

"You too, Emily."

Emily dished up dinner for herself and the girls. Her stomach was still doing flips, so she didn't eat much as she listened to the replay of Julia's and Claire's day. Both had good days and nothing much to report except the usual small spats with school friends and interesting facts learned by them in science.

***

Claire and Julia settled quickly and were now sleeping off their days, dreaming of tomorrow and fantasylands. Emily settled herself on the bed – hot, fruity tea in a mug on her bedside table, laptop, and a novel on the top of her down comforter. She wasn't sure if she was going to be in the mood to do either after talking to Andrea.

"Hey! How are you?" Andrea said once she picked up. She always made Emily smile with her abundant energy and to the point, positive nature.

"I'm pretty good," Emily said. "How was your Monday?"

"Oh, you know… The usual: work, daughter, dinner, wine, bed at some point."

Both women laughed and agreed on the monotony that their days held. After exchanging similar stories about the weekend chores and keeping up with all that needed to be done, Emily took a deep breath.

"What are you up to this weekend?" she asked casually while twisting the tassel of a crocheted blanket around her finger.

"Not much at all. The plan was just to hang out here. Mackenzie and I thought that we might try to do an entire thousand-piece puzzle in one weekend."

"Sounds like fun. Would you be able to watch the girls on Saturday evening then?"

"That would be fun! What do you have planned?" Andrea asked slyly, curiosity clear in her voice, "Do you finally have a hot date?"

"Actually, yes," Emily replied, hoping but not hoping Andrea would just guess and already know what she was going to tell her.

"Oh! Who's the lucky guy?"

"Izzy," Emily replied simply,

"Izzy?" Andrea asked after a few moments.

"Yes."

"My Izzy?"

"Yes."

"Emily? You're going out with Izzy?"

"Yes. Andrea —"

"Oh, Emily! I had a feeling about you, but I wasn't so sure, and when you were okay with coming to the bar with me, I wasn't too sure, but I knew it! I'm so happy you and Izzy are hitting things off! Why didn't you tell me sooner?"

"You're not upset with me for not telling you?"

"Not at all! You just came out of a messy marriage with, what I now assume, are some pretty complicated situations. You don't have to worry about me at all! I'm excited for you!"

"Oh, Andrea! Thank you for understanding. I'm sorry for not telling you sooner. I didn't know how to bring it up. You're right, there are so many complicated and really fucked up stories to share with you. I guess we're going to have to get together ourselves soon."

"Please don't worry at all. I'm happy that you're finally able to tell me. I know it was tough for Izzy, too. I've known a few of her friends who have come out as well, and it hasn't exactly been a clean break from what everyone else considers to be the norm."

"I haven't exactly told anyone else yet. Not that I don't want people to know. It just hasn't come up. Going out with Izzy will be kind of like a coming out message to the world, I guess."

Emily laughed nervously as she realized she was going out on her first openly gay date ever. She didn't have to hide; she didn't need to cover up her stares or hold back if she wanted to touch Izzy. She could finally be herself. The thought made Emily almost giddy.

"Are you okay if I drop the kids off around three? I'd like to go do some shopping quick before I meet Izzy."

"I'm totally good with that! You have to promise me a more detailed conversation about your life pre-me, though."

"Of course." Emily laughed again, feeling lighter the more she talked. It was as though a weight had been lifted off her shoulders. "Why don't you bring the girls over and stay for dinner on Sunday?"

"Perfect! See you Saturday!"

Emily sat in the dark. She'd never really told anyone about her feelings for other women before tonight. At least not outside of what her and Anika's relationship was. Emily felt a pang of guilt as she thought of her former partner.

She hadn't told her about Izzy yet. She worried that Anika would sever their friendship, at least for a while, once she found out Emily was possibly seeing someone. She sipped her tea in silence. Then she picked up her phone to text Izzy.

Hey! I talked to Andrea tonight, and she was over the moon about you and me going to dinner. She's going to keep the girls overnight. Do you want to meet at my place or yours, then take a cab to the restaurant?

Emily turned her ringer off and went to bed. She was excited and nervous about the date. She was emotionally charged, and it had been a long time since she had been with anyone.

She had her baggage from her long ago past and more recent events. In the end, Emily hoped she could keep her composure and hide what she didn't want Izzy to see.

Why do I want to hide who I am?

It worried Emily that she was falling into the same pattern with Izzy as she had in all her other relationships. She didn't want to play victim, and she didn't want to hold back who she was today and in the past.

Either Izzy would be okay with it or she wouldn't. Emily wouldn't dwell on it, but she wouldn't hide it any longer either. It was time for her to finally be the person she was always meant to be. She would finally be open and free.

CHAPTER 19

Emily woke to the increasing volume of her alarm. Rolling over to shut it off, she groaned and got out of bed. She showered and stood in front of her closet in her underwear when Julia groggily came into her bathroom.

"I don't want to go to school today," she proclaimed as she teetered on the toilet trying to stay still, her toes not quite reaching the ground yet.

"You have to go to school today, sweetie. It's your sharing day."

"I still don't want to. I want to stay home with you all day."

"I know, sweetie, but Mommy has lots of work to do, and I have to go have that meeting with Daddy at the courthouse."

Emily was still trying to decide what to wear. She needed to dress professional and classy, but also soft and give the allure of being a mom. She needed to make it clear that she was put together and comfortable, a good caregiver.

She crossed her arms over her chest as she stared at her wardrobe. Finally, she decided on a grey skirt with a white blouse and black closed-toe flats.

"You will have a great day at school, and tomorrow you're going to have a sleepover at Andrea's, then they're going to have dinner here on Sunday. How does that sound?"

"Are you sleeping over, too?"

"No, Mommy is going to go out for a bit with Izzy."

"I like Izzy," Julia said washing her hands and turning to wrap her small arms around Emily's waist.

Emily crouched down and returned Julia's hug, taking in the comfort of her daughter. She closed her eyes to soak it all in. "I like Izzy, too. I love you, Julia. Go get dressed and wake your sister up nicely, okay?"

Julia nodded and skipped off to her bedroom. Emily heard the yell from Claire as Julia flipped on the light and started rummaging through drawers looking for the perfect outfit for the day, all the while singing loudly.

Emily sighed and turned to the mirror to do something with her hair and face. She put her makeup on, then blow-dried her hair into light curls framing her face. Brushing her teeth and finishing with light lipstick, Emily shut the lights off and went to help the girls make their lunches. To her surprise, the girls had their lunches in their backpacks and were dressed and eating breakfast.

"Good morning." Emily kissed each of their heads and made a cup of coffee. "You both look like you had good sleeps."

"We get to sleep at Andrea's tomorrow?" Claire asked through a mouthful of Rice Krispies.

"Wait until your mouth is empty, Claire, but yes."

"Where are you going?"

"I'm going to go out for dinner with Izzy." Emily added flavored creamer to her coffee and sipped the hot beverage. It warmed her hands and mouth while the rest of her body heated up at the thought of Izzy.

"Why can't we go, too?" Julia whined, taking her bowl to the counter.

"Put it in the dishwasher, please," Emily reminded. "Because, just Izzy and I are going. We're going to have some adult time. Besides, you guys will have a blast at Andrea's."

"Ookay, Mom," Julia sulked.

"Time to get your shoes on. The bus will be here in five minutes." Emily brought their backpacks and helped with their coats. Kissing them both as they left, Emily shut the door and took a deep breath.

8:15. I have enough time to go over the documents again before I head to the courthouse.

Emily took the documents out of her briefcase and began to pour over them for what felt like the millionth time during the past few weeks. The court date had come quickly, apparently Conrad was in a hurry to get this sorted out. *Funny how he wasn't in a hurry to follow through on pre-arranged visitation for the sake of the girls, though.*

Emily listed off all the accusations Conrad had made about her and made sure to say out loud the responses for each one. She could feel her anger rise as she realized how foolish she had been ever to even date him in the first place.

She kicked herself repeatedly for not seeing the warning signs, but she now realized that he manipulated her and fed off her empathy and kindness. He needed to be saved, and she was in the business of trying to save souls like his.

I wouldn't have my girls if it weren't for him, though. And I wouldn't have met Anika, either. The path taken may not always be the one we intend, but we always end up where we are supposed to be.

Emily texted Anika while she reviewed her materials.

I'd love to chat if you have the time.

She wasn't sure if she'd receive a response. Anika avoided her since Conrad initiated the custody proceedings. After her lunch with Matisse, Emily saw a different picture of what was happening in her old neighborhood. It wasn't the clear-cut support that she thought she had when she left.

Emily put the papers away and snapped her briefcase closed. Shutting the lights off and grabbing the tea she had made while making her coffee, she locked the door behind her and made her way to her car.

***

The courthouse was so busy that Emily had trouble finding a parking spot. Paying the meter and rushing into the courtroom, Emily spotted her attorney in the back row.

"How's it going so far? I don't see Conrad or his lawyer anywhere."

"Last I saw, they were using one of the conference rooms. I met with Conrad's lawyer. He agrees that he's out to lunch on his demands. I know we've talked about what he's accusing you of. You need understand that there might be an investigation based on his claims. Is there anything else besides what you've told me that I need to know before we proceed?"

Emily hesitated. Her excitement about tomorrow night's date was now starting to feel more like stress than a chance to get to be herself. "I think I'm a lesbian, and I have a date with a woman tomorrow night," Emily blurted out. She blushed and looked around to see if anyone had heard her say 'lesbian' out loud.

Emily's lawyer looked at her, her mouth open for a moment. "Does Conrad know?"

"I don't think so …"

"Does anyone else know? Have you had relationships with women beforehand?"

"Well … kind of … I mean … It's a bit of a long story. I honestly don't think he knows about that stuff. And I don't think my personal life has anything to do with him. I haven't even officially come out, and none of what he's accused me of is even the slightest bit true."

"If he does know, and he brings it up, then it may provide an example of your character and trustworthiness. Did you cheat on him while you were together?" Her lawyer whispered, making notes in a notebook.

"Well … that's not why I left him. And he certainly didn't have any idea," Emily blushed and whispered.

"Emily …"

"I didn't think it was important. He hasn't given me an indication that he thinks –"

Emily was cut off when her attorney stood up as their case was called. She watched Conrad and his lawyer enter the courtroom together and sit down. Emily's stomach flipped, and she felt a cluster headache start as she began to stress about what effect the today's outcome would have on her life.

"I am, quite frankly, tired of seeing cases such as this," the judge started in without a clear word to either side. "Mr. Eckhart, you've made some very harsh accusations against your wife. Accusations that seem to be bordering on slander. Mrs. Eckhart, you've countered with logical explanations, but honestly, I feel like you're trying to keep the kids from your husband by not giving him the choice of weekends and expecting him to change his work schedule."

Emily looked at her lawyer angrily. Had they not understood the gravity of how Conrad had been with the girls. Wasn't she clear about why Emily needed to limit their time with him?

"You are both grown adults, and the fact that so many of you end up in this courtroom without the ability to figure out what might be best for the kids is beyond me. So, here's what I am mandating to happen: Both parties, including the girls, will go to counselling. Strict documentation will be made regarding these sessions, and there will be follow up on the expectations and work that needs to be done. You will both attend a co-parenting class.

"I have also designed a schedule of visitation for Mr. Eckhart. Given your position, I have given Mrs. Eckhart majority custody.

"Mrs. Eckhart, that doesn't mean you have the right to keep his children from him. Within the schedule I have set out who will drive the children to and from the visitation, and it is to be very strictly adhered to.

"Mr. Eckhart, I would suggest you be far more careful when accusing people with serious claims that you have. And just so you know, if every mother who had a couple of glasses of wine after a difficult day with the kids was considered a raging alcoholic, then we'd be living in a world full of them. I don't want to see either of you back in here."

Emily nodded to the judge then stepped around the table. "What was that about?" She whispered to her lawyer.

"This judge has very little patience for couples who try to throw the other under the bus. He doesn't waste time listening to the bickering and tends to just mandate a plan from the get-go. Saves a lot of court time and money in the long run."

"Hmm. I'm interested to see the schedule he laid out."

"I'll pick it up from the recorder's office and meet you in the lobby."

Emily nodded her approval and walked in search of the washroom. Taking her phone out of her purse, she sent off a quick text to Andrea letting her know she was done and that she'd call later to let her know what went on.

Emily hesitated for a moment then texted Anika for the second time that day. Though she seemed distant, she still felt a need to connect and share with her friend.

Hey Anika. Just wanted to let you know that the custody hearing was today. The judge wasn't happy with us being in court and pretty much told Conrad his accusations were unrealistic. I haven't seen the court's plans, but I get the feeling the judge was pretty 50/50. I'd love to chat soon … It's been too long. Love you. Xoxo

Emily looked at the text for a moment before sending it.

She had mixed feelings on what was going on between the two of them and what was going on in the rest of her life. Although it had been months since her romantic tryst with Anika, Emily still felt like she wasn't being fair to her.

Yet, Anika had made it quite clear she needed to make that distance from Emily. A part of her had held onto the possibility that maybe, just maybe, Anika would have the nerve to leave Matisse and finally be with her.

Shaking her head at her reflection in the mirror as she washed her hands, Emily smiled lopsided and allowed herself to feel relieved that today was over, that there would be a clear plan in place regarding the kids and Conrad, and that she had allowed herself to book a wonderful date for tomorrow night. Leaving the bathroom, she turned toward the lobby when someone grabbed her by the arm.

"You didn't win, you skank," a woman's voice spoke from behind Emily before she had a chance to turn around.

"Excuse me?" Emily turned to see Becka standing with her arms crossed. Anger and embarrassment flooded Emily as she remembered their first encounter at Susan's party.

"You heard me. Conrad's not a bad guy, and the fact you're playing him against his children is disgusting."

"I'm not sure we're talking about the same Conrad, but

the one I know was a terrible husband and has never done much in the way of building a healthy relationship with his children. I've never played our children against him. Ever. Plain and simple. Though, I know he'd tried to do it to me. I've witnessed it firsthand." Emily stood straight and stared hard at Becka.

"I suppose if you'd been a better wife, less concerned with yourself and more concerned with keeping your husband happy and keeping your family together, maybe you'd still have a marriage."

"I suppose, maybe if he'd been supportive, helpful, and not a prick, it could have gone that way, too ..." Emily tried hard to keep her cool. She shifted her purse between hands and crossed her arms just as her lawyer came up beside her.

"Emily ... now's maybe not a good time."

Emily looked at her lawyer, then back at Becka. Giving her attorney a sideway glance, she turned to go.

"What the hell is she doing here?" she whispered to her lawyer as they walked away.

"She drove in with Conrad this morning. You know her?"

"Not well. She'll sure have a hell of a surprise once she gets to know Conrad a little." Emily laughed at the thought of that done up woman having to look after him. Either she was going to tire of it rather quickly, or maybe he would. Emily changed the subject and asked, "What does the court order say?"

"You guys had already agreed upon most of it, such as holidays and birthdays. The judge ordered Conrad to pay you a percentage of child support, and you must share the responsibility of driving the girls to a central meeting place for all pick up and drop off, which the judge has planned out for the next six months.

"In my opinion, he'd have been better off keeping what you had offered as opposed to bringing you to court. Along with the when and the where, he's lain out the counseling and parenting sessions as well. Looks like you're going to be even busier over the next few months than you already are."

Emily took the documents from her lawyer and scanned them, looking through the schedule that had been laid out. "There was nothing unfair about what I had laid out. He made both of our lives more difficult by bringing it here."

"I agree; however, be aware … just because this was court-ordered doesn't mean he's going to follow it. You need to make a decision as to what your course of action will be if he doesn't follow this."

"He's going to take it and do what he wants with it. It won't matter to him. He's still going to do what he wants to do. Want to bet he doesn't make even one child support payment?" Emily raised an eyebrow and waved the documents around.

"You need to let me know how you want to proceed if things don't go as outlined," her lawyer said as they reached the exit. "You need to stick to your portion, and you need to inform me of any deviation from what has been ordered as soon as it happens."

"I just want the best for the girls. I want less drama and bullshit. They deserve better than he's ever been." Emily felt tears build as she realized that this was a finalization of sorts for her and Conrad's relationship.

"It will be okay, Emily. You're a great mom, and I know for a fact you have nothing but their absolute best interests at heart."

"Thank you," Emily said, taking a tissue from her purse and dabbing under her eyes. She wasn't about to let anyone who might be connected to Conrad see her break down in the courthouse. "I'll keep in touch."

Her lawyer smiled and opened the door for Emily as she stepped out into the cool air. She walked slowly to her car, ignoring her phone as several text messages went off in her purse. She didn't want to talk to anyone right now.

Emily felt like she was mourning. She was saying goodbye to something she still held out hope would fix itself or that she could fix. She climbed into the SUV and rested her head on the steering wheel, letting out hard sobs.

She cried for a long time while vehicles drove by and people walked past, none the wiser that she was allowing herself to fall apart so publicly.

The text messages had stopped, but the ringing of her phone brought her back to where she was. Looking at the caller ID, she saw it was Izzy. Taking a deep breath, she wiped her face with the back of her hand and answered.

"Hi, Izzy."

"Hi, Emily. How are you holding up?"

"I'm okay." Emily didn't elaborate. She suddenly felt uncomfortable talking to Izzy. She was feeling defeated and as though relationships were all doomed to fail. Talking to her right now wasn't really what she wanted to be doing. *Why did I answer?* The silence seemed to fall heavily between them; something that hadn't happened before.

"I just thought I'd check in." Izzy didn't press for details. "I'll see you tomorrow."

"Thanks. See you tomorrow." Emily hung up and looked at her phone. Tears started to stream down her face again as thoughts of Izzy, Conrad and Anika flooded her mind. Wiping them away, she started her car and left for her apartment.

CHAPTER 20

Emily got home and turned the music up loud. She didn't want to be alone with her thoughts any more today. Stripping out of her professional clothes, she danced around in only her panties.

She was belting out 'I Will Survive' when there was a knock on her door. Grabbing her robe from the back of her bedroom door, she turned down the music and opened the door. Standing there was a delivery man with a bouquet of mixed flowers.

"Are you Emily Eckhart?" the delivery man asked.

"Yes."

"Sign here, please." Emily signed and thanked the man then closed the door. Bringing the bouquet to the counter, she looked for a card or marking that might indicate who it was from. Tucked deep in the middle of the bouquet was a handmade paper card in purple with forget-me-nots set into the paper. Written in careful script were the words: *You've got this.* There were no other words, no signature, nothing. Emily smiled shyly and eyed the bouquet as she took out a vase.

Who could have sent it? There were only a couple of people she thought would send her flowers and only a few people who even knew about today.

Emily took a crystal tumbler out of the cabinet and poured a two-finger drink of almond tequila. She took a deep sip, refilled the glass, and buried her nose in the flowers. The sweet scent of the deep purples, pinks and blues filled her senses.

She stood back, her arms across her chest once again, then went back to the living room to turn the music back up. She threw on an old t-shirt and decided today would be a great day to get her house cleaned up. She wasn't sure what would happen with Izzy tomorrow night, but she didn't want to risk bringing her home to a messy house. Emily stopped for a moment and shook her head, realizing she was falling back into the same old mindset as before.

My outward appearance doesn't determine who I am. I'm more than my house, clothes, or job. Emily smiled to herself, "I am enough!" she said loudly as she swept, vacuumed, and wiped her away around her apartment.

She finished cleaning before the girls got home, so she decided to make them banana bread as snack. She was just pulling the loaves out of the oven when the girls came through the door. Turning around with a big smile on her face, she realized they weren't alone. Conrad had come through the door with them.

Emily, suddenly feeling naked in her t-shirt and spandex shorts, crossed her arms over her braless chest and stood straight.

"What are you doing here?" she asked firmly, hoping to come across as unimpressed and confident when she was really shaking inside.

"I just wanted to see the girls. I didn't have my visitation last week. I missed them." Conrad didn't look good. He was pale and expressionless, his arms hanging limply at his sides as he plainly explained himself.

"Didn't you read the court order, Conrad? You get the kids next weekend. I drive them to you on Friday."

"I'm working."

"You can't just show up whenever you want to. You're the one who wanted to go to court and didn't feel we could work it out on our own. I thought what I had given you was more than fair. I didn't ask you for anything. I never have."

Emily turned to the girls who had taken their stuff off but were standing between Emily and Conrad. "Girls," she said as she motioned to their room, "go put your stuff away in your bedroom and close your door. I'll come get you in a few minutes, okay?"

"I don't want to, Mom," Claire complained.

"It's not a choice. Your dad and I need to have a conversation."

Emily picked up the girls' backpacks and carried them to their room. The girls dragged themselves to their bedroom behind Emily. She closed the door behind her and spoke to her daughters in hushed tones. "I need to have a very serious conversation with your dad. I need you both to stay in here and keep your music on, okay?"

The girls nodded, and Emily pulled her phone from under her shirt. Hesitating, she briefly group-texted her lawyer and Andrea to outline what was going on. Giving the girls kisses, she left the room. She waited until she could hear the CD Claire had gotten for her birthday last year playing loudly before she moved toward Conrad.

"You can't be here. It isn't fair to the girls, it isn't fair to me, and you're violating what the order said. It doesn't matter if you miss your visitation or not. You can't just do what you want!"

Conrad took a step toward Emily. She stepped back, suddenly regretting not keeping the bar between herself and her ex-husband.

"It isn't too late, you know, Emily. You and I can still be together. We owe it to the kids to stay together. This isn't fair to them." Conrad still showed little emotion, his blank eyes staring at her.

"I can't do this, Conrad. We're not doing this. I've told you repeatedly that I'm done. There isn't going to be any reconciliation. You keep making my point. The things you said about me in the court papers, the lies you've told, even coming here today. You don't think the rules apply to you at all."

"I didn't say anything untrue. It needed to be out. I still love you. Don't you love me?"

"Conrad, it has nothing to do with love."

"You're not being fair to the kids by keeping them away from me." Conrad took two more steps in her direction.

Emily's phone rang. She jumped, then reached behind her to see who was calling. It was Andrea.

"Hi," she said as she made her way around to the other side of the bar.

"Are you okay, Emily?" Andrea asked quickly, concern flooding her voice. "Is he still there?"

"Yes, he's still here."

"Do you want me to call the police?"

Emily paused. Did she want to get the police involved? Was it worth it? The last months had taught her that she needed to let go of what she couldn't do and trust those with the skills to do what they needed to do.

I'm out of my league here. He needs to know this isn't okay.

"Yes," she answered.

Andrea hung up, and Emily put her phone down on the counter. She could still hear the music in the girls' room. She was glad they were listening to her and not trying to intervene. Emily was unsure what Conrad was capable of. There had been some scary moments when she was married. Moments that made her question who he really was.

"Does your lawyer know you're here?" Emily asked.

Conrad didn't respond. He stared at her blankly, his face slightly pouty, eyes dark.

"I don't know what to tell you, Conrad. There's nothing to discuss. The court decided it for us. That was what you wanted, wasn't it?"

"I wanted you, Em. I wanted my life back." He started to walk toward the end of the bar. "You were my life. I gave you everything –"

"You gave me nothing but a bunch of headaches, Conrad. You did nothing to help me before or after we had the girls. The only thing you were concerned about was you."

"I love you. You're my world. Do you realize that? Do you realize what you've done to me?" Conrad started to cry. He walked around the bar and Emily moved away. She reached the end of the kitchen where she couldn't go any further. She now cursed herself for letting him get behind where she thought she would be safe.

"I loved you, too, Conrad. But I deserved more. The girls deserved more. I couldn't raise them with the example you provided. It was setting them up for failure to watch their father treat their mother so disrespectfully."

Conrad didn't respond. He just moved closer. Emily stood straight with her arms wrapped across her chest. He stopped about a foot from her. She could smell his body and his breath. Her stomach lurched and felt sick. She struggled to stay calm as he stood in front of her, towering eight inches taller than she was.

He inched closer still and leaned his head down to hers. He tried to kiss her lips and she turned her head away, her eyes shut tight.

"Don't do this." Emily tried to sound firm, but her voice and body shook. She hated being so close to him. She hated how he smelled and how he breathed loudly in her ear and tried to nibble her ear lobe. Her body repulsed at his touch. Emily cheeks were hot with flowing tears.

Suddenly there was a sharp knock on the door. Emily didn't answer, and another knock erupted loudly.

"Police! We have a call about a domestic disturbance."

The door opened, and two police officers stepped in, scanned the area, and spotted the confrontation in the kitchen.

Conrad stepped back from Emily slightly and looked at the officers, then back at Emily. Putting on a smile, he said, "Everything is good here, officers. You must have the wrong apartment."

"Emily?" the female officer asked, hand on her weapon. "Are you okay?"

Emily nodded then looked toward the girls' bedroom. The officer followed her look and saw the door to the girls' bedroom open slightly and four little eyes peaking out. "Hi girls," the officer spoke softly. "Do you mind if we shut that door again? We're just going to have a little talk with your mommy and daddy, okay?"

The girls looked towards Emily, and she nodded and smiled weakly. The girls closed the door and the female officer positioned herself between the door and the kitchen.

"Conrad?" the male officer asked. "Why don't you step out here and we can have a little chat, okay?"

"I don't really think we need to do that. Everything here is fine. Right, Emily?"

Emily didn't look at Conrad. She kept her eyes fixed on the female officer and the door. She didn't want the girls to see any more than they had to.

"Tell them everything is fine, Emily," Conrad said more firmly, now through gritted teeth.

"Conrad. We're going to need you to come with us, okay? Let's go talk about this downstairs."

Conrad looked from Emily to the officers again. He shrugged and walked out of the apartment, glaring at Emily as he did.

Once the door was shut, Emily let out a sob. The female officer led Emily to the couch and covered her with a blanket. Emily recited the courthouse events and when Conrad appeared. She felt numb.

"Has he ever done anything like this in the past?" the officer asked, taking notes as Emily spoke.

"Umm…" She was still struggling with the fake loyalty that she felt to Conrad. Years of gaslighting and emotional abuse had taught her to protect him, but she finally knew better. She decided to be open and tell everything that had happened.

She recounted instance after instance of the emotional, mental, and sometimes physical abuse that she and the girls had endured. She included the time when Conrad took the girls from school. She didn't want to protect someone who could hurt her or her daughters any longer. It wasn't worth it.

Just as Emily finished telling her story, Andrea came through the door with Mackenzie in tow. She ran to Emily on the couch, indicating for Mackenzie to go find Claire and Julia in their bedroom. Andrea sat with her arm around Emily and hugged her. She let her head fall onto Andrea's shoulder and more tears came as the officer finished her notes.

"Do you want to press charges?"

"I … I don't know. I just want this to stop. I want better for my daughters," Emily sobbed, the effort to wipe the tears away futile.

"I'm going to file a case with the family courts to change what the judge had given during your custody hearing. A social worker will be in contact with you. As of right now, he will have no contact with them. A judge needs to decide on the next steps.

"Emily, you need to fight it this time. You can't let his manipulative behaviour have your concerns thrown out of court again. You have options. Supervised visitations and a restraining order might be the best way to go with this."

Emily nodded, crying harder as the thought of him taking the girls overwhelmed her with the possibility that she may not ever see them again if that happened. "Thank you." Emily tried to smile.

"It will be okay." The officer placed a reassuring hand on Emily's shoulder and smiled.

Emily fell into Andrea and let herself cry until she felt small arms around her. Breaking away from Andrea, she saw Claire and Julia holding tight to her, tears streaking their faces as well. "I love you, girls. So very much." She sobbed into their heads.

Taking a shaky, deep breath, Emily sat up and broke away from all the arms around her. "Seems to me like we should probably order some pizza, and a funny movie might be in order. What you do girls think?"

The girls jumped up and down and cheered. Andrea squeezed Emily's hand and stood. "Why don't you go have a shower and I'll order the pizza, okay?"

Emily stood and nodded, then walked to her bathroom and shut the door. Shaking, she slid down to the floor and, knees up, she let her head fall into her arms. She sobbed for several minutes then stood under the hot shower. Drying off, she chose an oversized sweater and leggings. Checking her phone before leaving her room, Emily noticed she had two missed calls and five text messages.

One call was from her lawyer. She wanted to know what had happened. Emily called her back and explained the situation and what the officer had said.

"I'll make sure to file a grievance with Conrad's lawyer immediately and get the paperwork going for a custody change. He can't have the kids alone."

"Thank you."

The second call was from Anika. She sounded upset and worried. One of the text messages was from her as well. Emily called her back.

"What's going on?" Anika asked. "I got a call from Conrad who said you'd had him arrested."

"He wouldn't leave and was acting threateningly. He didn't have any right to be here. I didn't have any other choice." Emily sat on the edge of her bed playing with a frayed edge on the bottom of her sweater.

"It was a pretty tough day for both of you, Emily. I'm sure he just needed to a little support."

"It was more than that, Anika. What is going on with you? I just had to call the police and have Conrad arrested because he wouldn't leave MY apartment after he tried to drag me through the mud in court. You haven't returned my phone calls or texts for weeks."

"Nothing is going on. Conrad is alone, and it seems like you're deliberately trying to make things harder for him. I know things weren't great when you guys were together. I one hundred percent support your leaving him, but I'm his friend, too. It's just been hard to see him taking you leaving so hard."

Emily was shocked. She always thought Anika was on her side. She believed that, out of all the people she once knew, the woman she shared a bed with for four years would support and help her when it came to Conrad. Anika had said as much when they were together. It didn't seem to be the case any longer.

Emily felt herself start to fume. She was past the point of crying any more today, now she was just angry, "I can't believe you're saying this after everything we've been through. After everything I told you about him and how you saw him treat me."

"Sometimes you just need to get past things, Emily."

"What the hell is going on, Anika?" Emily asked, "Seriously!"

"What's going on with you, Emily? Anything you feel like telling me, or are you keeping more than just what was really going on with Conrad from me?"

Emily inhaled sharply. She hadn't told Anika about Izzy yet. It just hadn't seemed like the right time. Emily was worried about hurting Anika and afraid of losing her friendship. *But what did Anika expect?*

Anika had been very clear that she would have a hard time getting through the period when Emily decided to start seeing anyone. Emily hadn't intended to start seeing anyone, but she had happened upon Izzy, and she was too wonderful of a person to not have in her life. "If you have something you want to ask me, Anika, then just ask it."

"Are you seeing someone?" Anika asked bluntly

"Not officially. No. But there is a woman whom I've gone to dinner with a few times and we've had coffee." Emily hesitated. She didn't really feel she owed her any specific details. Anika was the one who said she'd had no intentions of ever leaving Matisse. After all, she strung Emily along and kept her on the back burner for her use when she wanted it, with little concern for Emily or how it affected her.

"You told me you'd be honest when you found someone."

"I didn't lie to you. It's not serious. Besides, how about you? You promised me you'd make efforts to come here more, that you wanted to be with me. Instead, you've decided to fix your marriage and keep me as a side."

"I've always told you that *us* was for Matisse and me. Even when I said I wanted to be with you, which I always wanted, I was honest that my marriage was still important to me. You haven't been honest at all."

"Things aren't always what they seem." It was clear Anika had no idea about Matisse's continued advances. She didn't want to hurt Anika, nor did she want to break her and Matisse up.

Furthermore, Emily was no longer sure of her feelings. The dull ache of yearning was still there, but it wasn't as much of a need now. Just something familiar and comforting.

She and Anika knew each other. They knew each other's bodies, their emotions, the buttons to push to piss off or turn each other on. But Emily wasn't sure it was the life-long love she had hoped for.

She was finally coming to terms with the fact that going from relationship to relationship gave her no chance to grow as herself.

"I have to go, Anika. I'd like to talk to you about this more. It's been a long day, and I need to go and be with the girls."

"Maybe," Anika's short reply hurt Emily more than anything else she had said tonight.

Emily hesitated. She wanted to tell Anika she loved her, but once again wondered if it was because she loved her like that or if it was out of habit.

She walked into the living room. Andrea was just setting plates out and the girls had opened the pizza and were eyeing up their favorites. Glasses of juice littered the table and there was a movie that was paused while the girls dished up.

Andrea noticed Emily standing at the doorway and went to her. Emily let herself fall into her friend, though she held her tears in. She was tired of crying and wanted to show her girls that she could be strong in the face of what was going on around them.

Smiling at Andrea, she went to Julia and kissed her.

"I love you, momma," she said in her little voice.

"I love you, sweetie." Emily kissed Claire's head and hugged her close to her. "I love you, Claire."

"Love you, Mommy."

Andrea motioned to Emily to meet in the kitchen. Emily stood where she had been just an hour ago, hoping that the counter would keep her safe. She looked around and took a shaky breath. Then, she grabbed two wine glasses from the cupboard and poured for Andrea and herself. She gently pushed Andrea's glass across the counter and took a deep swallow of hers.

"Are you doing okay?" Andrea asked.

"I don't know. I think I'm okay. I think part of me knew that this was coming, but I ..." Emily trailed off, looking around again and feeling hot tears form as she relived Conrad's breath on her neck and the feel of him so close to her.

"It just feels less safe now. Here feels less safe. This place was somewhere I didn't have any memories of him, and now I have this ..." She motioned around the room then dropped her hand to her side and gave Andrea a defeated look.

"It will be okay. You've been in contact with your lawyer, and now his behaviour is on record with the police. Maybe drive the girls to school and pick them up for the next little bit. It will help you keep a closer eye on them. The girls will know that he's not a safe person to go with, and you can let the school know that he shouldn't be there, either. If you need my help, I can be there as well. Just let me know what you need."

"Thank you." Emily gave Andrea a sideways smile then drank more of her wine. "At least everything he tried to say about me in court will probably become crap considering his response to all of this."

"I agree. I think you'll be granted full custody with very few supervised visits."

"Yeah." Emily window on the opposite side of the apartment. The lights twinkled outside, and she could see a thin line of traffic make its way down a hill.

The sound of the phone pulled her from her trance. Looking at the display she realized it was Izzy. Emily tossed Andrea a look, and her friend smiled as she sipped her wine. Emily excused herself to answer.

"Are you doing okay? Andrea texted me to say there had been an issue with the girls' father."

"I'm okay. It was a bit tense, and I had to call the police, but things are settled down now."

VANESSA M. THIBEAULT

"I'm glad to hear that, Emily. If you need to take a rain check on dinner tomorrow, I'm okay with that. If you need to just be at home and be with your girls …" Izzy was full of emotion. Emily could hear the concern in her voice and breathed in deeply.

"I'm okay. I need some time out, I think. Away from here for the evening. I'm not sure I'm going to sleep so well tonight after what happened," Emily conveyed. *After what could have happened …*

She felt herself go cold at the thought of what might have occurred if the police hadn't shown up when they did. Or worse if Emily hadn't gotten a hold of Andrea when she had.

"Try to get some sleep. If you need to just call it an early night and sleep at Andrea's tomorrow night, that's okay, too." Izzy joked.

"Thank you, Izzy. I'll see you tomorrow. I promise."

Emily set her phone on her bed and went back to the living room. Finding Andrea on the couch with the kids, she snuggled in with the bunch and finished her wine while laughing at the movie and trying to forget the day.

CHAPTER 21

Emily woke early the next morning to the sound of someone at her door. She sat up in a panic, confused and disorientated. Looking at her clock, she realized it was already after eight.

She threw her robe on and ran her fingers through her hair as she walked to the door where another set of knocks erupted. Cautiously, Emily peeked through the peep hole to see Andrea standing there with the girls, cups in a drink holder, and bags of food.

Emily quickly opened the door and grabbed some of the items, "When did you go out?" Emily asked

"About an hour ago. You were sleeping so soundly I didn't want to wake you. The girls and I all snuck out to the park and then decided to hit up that amazing coffee shop just down the block. We couldn't decide what looked best, so we got a little bit of everything. The guy behind the counter said some of the pastries will freeze alright, too."

"Andrea …" Emily started, then she realized her stomach was growling. "Thank you."

She gave Andrea a one-armed hug as she opened one of the paper bags and took in the delicious smell of the muffins and pastries.

"Any time. Dig in! I'll grab plates for the girls."

Emily chose a cheese and chive scone and a raspberry Danish with cream cheese icing. Andrea had grabbed caramel lattes made with coconut milk and extra espresso shots as well, and Emily relished in being spoiled. The girls ate at the bar while Emily and Andrea got cozy on the couch with their breakfasts.

"I talked to Anika last night," Emily started. "Before I came out for pizza."

Andrea raised an eyebrow as she munched on a huge lemon poppyseed muffin. "You haven't talked to her much lately. Did you call her, or did she call you?"

"She called me. She got a call from Conrad at the police station." Emily took a tentative swallow of her latte and found it was just the right temperature. Taking a long sip of the rich liquid, Emily swallowed hard. "Things with Anika and I are complicated. Without getting into too much of the dirty details, we were together while I was still with Conrad. Since I moved away, things between her and I have been rather strained. We'd originally made plans to move away together and start a new life with our five kids, but she decided to rekindle things with her husband, and …" Emily shrugged, "I moved here."

"That explains a lot," Andrea stated. "I knew there was something more than just a friendship going on with you two, but I didn't want to pry. What did she say about Conrad's phone call?"

"She was mostly on his side. Kind of. She said she thought I took it too far by having the police involved, and that I hadn't given Conrad enough of a say when it came to seeing the kids. She was friends with both of us, and she said it was so she could keep me in the loop and make my life easier, but I'm not so sure now.

"I think she's acting out of hurt," Emily continued.

"Somehow, she found out that I have been hanging around Izzy, and I know it's hard for Anika to know that we aren't going to be together anymore, but …" Emily began to tear up. She took another long sip of her coffee in an effort to hold back emotions threatening to spill over once again.

"I think she has a lot of hurt and regret with you," Andrea said. "You're a wonderful person, and, when you guys were together, I could sense there was something very special between the two of you. However, you need to go on with your life and make the decisions that are best for you and your girls! You can't allow yourself to be held back by Conrad, Anika, or anyone for that matter. You deserve to be happy, Emily. You've had so much unhappiness in your life so far, you deserve a break." Andrea squeezed Emily's hand. Emily returned a half smile and finished her Danish with another swig of coffee.

"Did the girls say anything to you while you were out with them?"

"Julia asked if her dad was in trouble. I told her that you loved her and cared for her and her sister very much and that you make the best choices to keep them safe. I told them that their dad just needed to talk to the police for a little while so he could treat you better and you won't cry so much. I kind of rambled … I hope all of that was okay. I felt like a deer in the headlights." Andrea laughed and sighed deeply, blowing her hair out of her face as she took another big bite of muffin.

"No, that's just fine. I'm not sure there's a right way for any of this to be explained. I'm sure they're going to have lots of questions and probably bring the whole thing up a lot soon and, realistically, probably for a long time to come."

"True."

"I'll go to their school Monday to alert them. I'm not sure what their policies are. I do kind of worry about Conrad trying to get to them through the school."

"Call your lawyer, then go to the school with your own information. That way, everything is documented, and there won't be any way around what's allowed and what isn't."

"Good idea. I'll call her in a bit. Do you mind watching the girls while I do that? She called yesterday and I didn't call her back. I'm sure she's wondering what went on."

"No problem! I'll be right here. I'll get the girls going on some homework and reading. Then they don't have to worry about it tonight while they're at my house."

"Thanks, Andrea. You're the best."

Emily kissed the girls as she left the room. She closed her bedroom door quietly and dialed her lawyer. She picked up halfway through the first ring. "Emily! You should have called sooner. Are you doing okay? How are the kids handling it all?"

"They're okay. A little shook up, but they're resilient, if they're anything. I'm holding up okay. It was a bit of a long night. Have you heard from Conrad's lawyer? Has the judge said anything?"

"I spoke with Conrad's lawyer last night. He was as surprised as I was that Conrad came to your home. I haven't heard from the judge yet, but I have filed to have all custody removed from your ex until a later date when a full investigation can be done. I should hear later today if that went through or not. In the meantime, as far as I know, Conrad has headed back to work."

"That's good. Maybe getting away from all of this will help him come to his senses." Emily bit her lip nervously and bounced her knee up and down as she sat on the edge of the bed. "Do you think he'll come back again?"

"I'm not sure, Emily. I hope he's learned his lesson by being arrested. He was read the riot act at the police station, and hopefully, some of it sank in."

"I hope so."

"Are you free next week to meet with me and the social worker?"

"Yes. Oh, I was going to ask, what kind of information should I give the school?"

"We'll have custody papers early next week. This will clear up any questions about your custody and make it clear for the school administrators."

Emily shuddered at the thought of Conrad taking the girls from the school and not knowing where they could be. "Yeah," Emily mumbled. "Thanks again for all your work."

"That's my job. Now get some rest this weekend. The next few weeks are going to be tough."

"I'll try." Emily lay down on her bed and closed her eyes. She pulled the covers over her body and let herself relax. She just needed a few minutes alone to process.

CHAPTER 22

Emily woke to gentle hands on her shoulder and someone calling her name softly. Rolling over, she came face to face with Julia and Claire.

"Hi Mommy," they said together.

"Hi girls," Emily said groggily, sitting up. "What time is it?"

"After lunch. Andrea made us grilled cheese with lots of veggies and the watermelon that was there." Claire explained, climbing onto the bed for a snuggle.

"Andrea said we could come wake you up. That you'd probably like to get up soon." Julia chimed in, crawling in on the other side and placing her head on Emily's chest.

"Thanks, guys. Guess I should get up and dressed, hey?" Emily laughed and hugged both girls tightly to her, kissing each of their heads. "Do you still want to have a sleep over with Mackenzie?"

"Yeah!" they said together again.

"Can you come with us to Andrea's for a bit, too?" Julia asked, hugging Emily close.

"Of course. How about if I get Izzy to pick me up there. Then you can see her, too."

The girls nodded their approval, and each gave Emily a kiss before they bounced out of the bedroom to tell Andrea the news.

Emily stretched and got out of bed, straightening the sheets and comforter before she went to her closet to pick out something to wear for the evening. Setting an overnight bag on her bed, Emily tossed in some pajamas, underwear, a pair of jeans, burgundy knit sweater and a tankini.

A sudden panic came over her. Putting her hand on the wall to steady herself, she tried to catch her breath while tears streamed down her face.

She felt a hand on her shoulder. Emily jumped away from it, crying out. Andrea stood there with a cup of coffee and a concerned expression on her face.

"I'm not sure I should be going out tonight, Andrea ..." Emily wiped her nose and cheeks on her sweater sleeve.

"I think you need to go out and have fun," Andrea said. "I think a night away from this apartment will do you and he girls good. You don't have to stay out late, and you and Izzy are more than welcome to come back to my place and just hang out or watch a movie or whatever. The girls will be safe at my house, you won't have to worry about them." Andrea rubbed a sympathetic hand over Emily's shoulder again and handed her the coffee. "You need this."

Emily laughed and took a sip. "Where did you find Bailey's?" Emily took another long swallow of the creamy liquid that started to warm her from the inside.

"I grabbed it while we were out this morning. I thought you might end up needing a bit of a pick-me-up later." They both laughed while Andrea sat on the bed. "What are you wearing tonight?"

"I don't know. Nothing too crazy. The restaurant is nice, but not extravagant. I don't want to be too dressed up just in case we go for a drink somewhere else."

"True. What about your black jeggings with that oversized blue sweater that falls off one shoulder? You could wear your black boots. They're flats, so even if you guys decide to walk somewhere, you'll be comfortable."

"Good call! I knew I was friends with you for a reason." Emily winked and pulled the clothes Andrea mentioned out of the closet.

Andrea left to motivate the girls to clean up and pack their bags for the night while Emily got dressed and did her hair and makeup. She looked in the mirror. Her face in general and eyes were still a little splotched from crying. There wasn't much she could do about it right now, and she didn't want to put a ton of makeup on for fear of crying when she was with Izzy.

Deciding on simple, Emily applied a thin layer of cover up on the black circles under her eyes and put a thin layer of eyeliner on her top lid. She then added blue eyeshadow for an accent. Waterproof mascara finished the look, and she was done within five minutes. Next, she added some product and a little water to her hair, then blow dried until she had some natural volume.

Emily added the dandelion seed necklace her brother had sent her when she had left Conrad. He included a note that read, "Now you'll always have a place to keep your wishes safe." Nathan and Emily didn't talk often, and she made a mental note to call him and update him on the girls and her new life. She stopped for a moment and wondered how he would react to her change of lifestyle. She decided that he would love Izzy and anything that made Emily happy.

Grabbing boots from the top of her closet, Emily did a quick spritz with perfume and left the room.

Andrea was loading the dishwasher and putting away the last of the dish towels when Emily came out. Andrea looked up and she did a little twirl.

"You look great!" Andrea said with a smile. "The girls are about ready to go."

"You girls ready?" Emily asked, putting her boots on.

"You look pretty, Mom," Claire said. "And you smell good, too."

"Thanks, sweetie."

"I'll meet you at my place. See you soon," Andrea chimed as she left.

Suddenly alone with the girls in the apartment for the first time, Emily felt the panic rise in her chest. She picked up her bag and purse and nervously played with the scarf around her neck. Tapping her foot impatiently, Emily felt a small hand in hers and looked down to see Julia, coat and shoes on, looking at her. "I love you," she said in her small voice.

"I love you, too." Emily choked back tears then took a stand in her mind.

I'm a good mom. Conrad didn't break me before, I won't let him break me now. I still deserve to be happy.

"Let's go, girls!" Emily locked the door behind her, and they drove to Andrea's singing all their favorite songs as loud as they could.

***

Emily sipped her wine as she and Andrea laughed watching the girls play Twister. Their small bodies struggled to reach everywhere they were supposed to. It was entertaining to watch them twist and turn to make it work.

"I don't think my body bends like that anymore," Emily said while she refilled her and Andrea's glasses.

"You've just been out of the game for too long," Andrea joked and winked at Emily.

Emily playfully stuck her tongue out at Andrea and faked giving her glass of wine back. Andrea laughed and stuck her tongue out in return. Clinking their glasses together, they took sips as Izzy walked in.

Emily noticed the confident way she entered the room, her short hair styled back with volume, but her makeup was still simple: red lipstick and a little mascara.

She wore black and white striped leggings, black flats and a white blouse with a red scarf that matched her lip color.

Emily smiled as she caught Izzy's eye, and Izzy smiled back. Picking her way around the tangled mess of kids, Izzy sat on the arm of the couch beside Emily.

"How is everyone?" she asked, picking up a glass from the table and filling it with the remainder of the wine.

"I'm not sure I've ever actually witnessed a game of Twister. I've always played, and God knows it's been years since that!" Emily spoke up, taking in Izzy's rich and musky scent.

"The kids sure make it entertaining!" Andrea chimed in. Turning to Izzy, she asked, "How are you? Long week at work?"

"It wasn't too bad. I finished up with a couple of clients, so next week I will hopefully have some breathing room to do the things I've been pushing off, such as billing and email." Izzy laughed and rolled her eyes, sighing and swallowing a large gulp of her wine.

Feeling the effects of the wine already, Emily put her glass down and reached for her water. "What time were the reservations for again?"

"Seven-thirty," Izzy replied. "I'll call a cab in about ten minutes."

"Sounds great."

CHAPTER 23

The ride to the restaurant was quiet. Emily was nervous, and Izzy made small talk with the cab driver. Exiting the vehicle, they strolled toward restaurant together, Emily keeping a comfortable distance between her and Izzy, unsure of how she felt. This was a first for her, and the new territory was terrifying.

Emily watched Izzy as they walked. Her makeup was just right, and the clothes she had chosen hugged her slim figure in all the right places. Emily found herself becoming aroused and blushed. It had been a long time since she dated, let alone a true date with a woman. Her and Anika went out, but they had never had the chance to be themselves. They always pretended, hid their looks, and hushed their conversations.

Emily took a deep breath and allowed herself to take the risk and follow her heart. Closing the distance between them, she entwined her fingers with Izzy's. She turned with a gentle smile and gave Emily's hand a small squeeze as their hands closed around one another's.

They were quickly seated. Izzy had ordered a bottle of red wine to be tableside when they arrived, and they sipped the full-bodied Syrah in silence for a few minutes.

"Are you doing okay?" Izzy leaned forward and gazed intently at Emily. She reached across and slowly ran her hand down the other's forearm.

"I'm okay. The last few days seem so unreal still." Emily sipped her wine as she placed her hand in Izzy's, who, in turn, ran her thumb over Emily's knuckles. Emily felt herself redden and she met Izzy's eyes.

"So, what about you? What's new at your end of the city?"

Izzy smiled and sat back with her wine, taking her hand from Emily's, "Lots of long days the last two weeks. We're trying to make a bunch of deadlines with clients who change their minds every couple of days, and head office seems to think filling entry level positions while we're in the middle of it all isn't spreading us too thin."

"Funny how they never seem to ask the guys doing the work what would be best, hey?" Emily laughed and shook her head. "I'm thankful for the flexibility I have with my job. I still get to be a part of all the important things with the girls and make a decent living."

"You have the best of both worlds," Izzy replied warmly, gesturing with her wine glass. She cocked her head to one side. "Tell me about your family. We haven't talked much about them."

Emily drew in a breath and took a long swallow of her wine. "Well …" she began, "my family certainly isn't as close knit as yours. I have two younger sisters and an older brother. I had an older sister, but she died when I was twelve." Emily looked down at her lap, her hands entwined with each other as she thought of the family she had been estranged from for so long.

"I'm sorry, Emily. Do you talk to your siblings often?"

"Our relationship has gotten better over the last few years It was strained when I left home at sixteen. My sisters feel like I should have stayed."

"What about your brother?"

"Nathan is only my half-brother. We have the same dad. He came to live with us for a few months, about a year after my sister died. Our dad and he didn't get along so well," Emily paused thinking back on her tumultuous childhood. "Nathan stayed with us for six months. My dad said some cruel things about why he left, all of which I found out later weren't true. I finally went to live with my aunt in Regina and came back to BC after I graduated. I met Conrad soon after that."

"Do you still have contact with Nathan?" Izzy leaned forward, her brow furrowed.

"We chat every now and then, probably a few times a year. He's been trying to get my sisters and I together for a while now. I just haven't had the energy to go through everything with them."

"Conrad took a lot out of you, even before you left him."

"Yeah ..." Emily finished her wine and reached, palm up, fingers out and inviting. Izzy placed her hand in Emily's and squeezed.

Emily smiled, fingering her necklace with her other hand, "Right after I left Conrad, Nathan sent this necklace. I never fully confided in him about what was going on, but I think he knew. He never did like Conrad much."

"Big brother intuition I suppose."

Emily sighed and shook her head to dispel the negative. Pouring more wine for both, she raised her glass, "Here's to better times."

"To better times!" Izzy happily clinked with Emily as the server brought their meals.

"Have you and Andrea always been close?" Emily asked between mouthfuls of blackened tuna and salad.

"Not always. Siblings have their differences. There's five years between us, so I think that played a part."

"Siblings always have differences. I think sometimes people forget how hard it is to live with someone day in and day out!" Emily said.

"Agreed!"

They finished their meals and debated ordering a third bottle of wine. Laughing and finding a comfortable space with each other, they looked over the dessert menu. Emily stroked the back of Izzy's hand as the other read off the list of decadent desserts. She watched Izzy's mouth and studied her features.

God, she has a kissable mouth, Emily thought.

Izzy's looked brightly at Emily. In turn, she blushed and hoped Izzy couldn't read her thoughts.

"How about if we skip dessert here and take a cab back to my place?" Emily paused and then hastily added, "Just for a quiet cup of coffee or something."

"I'd like that," Izzy replied as she waved the server over. When she pulled out her wallet to pay, Emily put a hand on her arm.

"My treat, please."

"Emily —"

"You can buy next time."

"Is this your way of ensuring a second date?" Izzy asked, winking and putting her wallet away.

Emily texted Andrea as she waited outside the door for Izzy.

How are the girls? Just heading for a coffee, then we will be home.

Emily hesitated before pushing send. *Should I have told here where we're going?* She started to worry about how honest she should be with Andrea about starting a relationship with her older sister. Before she could doubt herself anymore, Andrea returned her text.

I hope that by 'coffee' you mean back to your place for quieter conversation and another drink. Girls are great. Everyone is sleeping. Go have fun, and don't worry about coming home early. Izzy has a key.

Emily laughed out loud at Andrea's straightforwardness. She shook her head and responded with a smiley emoji sticking out its tongue. Feeling a hand on her waist, she turned around to see Izzy smiling at her.

"What's so funny?" she asked.

"Andrea."

"Oh?" Izzy replied with a raised eyebrow.

"I told her we were going for coffee, and she said she hoped it was at my place ... for another drink."

"She is a funny one, that Andrea," Izzy paused and looked around. "I called a cab while I was inside. It should be here any minute."

***

The ride was short, and Emily felt butterflies start to flutter as they got out of the cab. They walked up to her apartment in silence.

I'm not sure I'm ready for this yet, Emily thought

"It smells wonderful in here," Izzy said as she unzipped her boots and set them beside her purse.

"Thanks. The girls found some awesome air fresheners that smell like baked cookies. Julia always complains that it makes her hungry."

"I have to agree with her on that one," Izzy replied, following Emily into the kitchen.

"Would you like a cup of coffee or a tea? I have wine and whiskey as well."

"What are you having?"

Emily stopped on the other side of the bar. "I was thinking a whiskey."

"Then I'll have one as well."

Emily held Izzy's eye for a moment. She felt herself flush with a warmth that spread throughout her body. A familiar ache started as she tore herself away from Izzy's green eyes, now darker since the start of the evening.

Steadying her hands, she took two crystal tumblers from the cupboard and poured generous helpings for each of them. "Ice?" she asked without turning around as she poured.

"Yes."

Emily retrieved the ice and exited the kitchen, motioning for Izzy to follow her to the living room. They sat on the couch with their legs crossed. Emily took a swallow of the strong beverage and let its comfort calm the nervous chills she tried to keep under control.

Izzy sipped her whiskey and ran a stockinged foot up the arch of Emily's. She laughed and her foot involuntarily kicked Izzy, almost causing her to spill her drink.

"I'm incredibly ticklish," Emily explained. "I'm not responsible for anything I do while being tickled."

"Noted," Izzy laughed and took another sip of her drink. Putting it on the table, she placed her hand on Emily's leg. Emily placed hers over it.

"Are you okay with this?" Izzy asked. "We don't have to do anything you're not comfortable with."

"I'm very okay," Emily whispered as Izzy's other hand traced her jaw. Emily closed her eyes and allowed Izzy's hands to trace down her cheekbone and across her jaw, pausing at her lips. Then she traced down Emily's neck and over a bare shoulder. Emily felt goose bumps all over and breathed heavily with arousal.

Emily opened her eyes to see Izzy's soft and hungry eyes. Beautiful lips pursed together, her body calm and relaxed. Emily reached out and placed a finger along Izzy's jaw and traced down her neck.

Then she stood, nodded toward the bedroom, and entwined her fingers with Izzy's. Emily could feel the heat from her body, and she tried to calm the rolling in her stomach. *It's been so long,* she thought.

Emily left the lights off, leaving the only illumination coming from the living room. She turned and placed a hand on Izzy's hip, feeling the curves under the leggings.

Emily pressed her cheek against Izzy's, who placed her hand on the small of Emily's back. Their lips slowly connected. The kiss was slow and tentative as they explored the new territory. Izzy slipped her tongue through Emily's slightly opened mouth, and Emily allowed a quiet groan to escape her lips. She met Izzy's tongue and opened her mouth wider to allow them more access.

Izzy placed her hand on the back of Emily's neck, deepening the kiss. Emily tensed and pulled away at the feel of Izzy's touch.

"I'm sorry," Izzy panted.

"No …" Emily closed her eyes to catch her breath. "I just …" Emily reached for Izzy.

"We don't have to do anything, Emily," Izzy stated, their foreheads together. She held Emily's hand under their chins and placed her other hand on the small of Emily's back. "There's no pressure. No expectations."

"I want to …" Emily was close to tears. "I just need to be slow. After Conrad … and I have a lengthy past … I'm sorry. If you don't want to. If you don't … If this doesn't work –"

Izzy silenced Emily by pressing their lips together. Then, she whispered, "There are no judgements from me. No expectations. We'll only do what you feel comfortable with."

"Thank you," Emily whispered as she returned Izzy's kiss with passion and vigor. She pulled Izzy closer to her bed and leaned back. They laughed as they fell on the soft comforter and kissed again.

Emily ran her hands down Izzy's hips and over the leggings. Then she put her hands inside their waistband and tentatively pulled them down to reveal a light purple thong.

Emily groaned as she became more aroused at her discovery. "Izzy …"

Izzy stepped out of her leggings and replied with deep and trailing kisses down Emily's neck. In turn, she unbuttoned Izzy's blouse and slipped it off. Izzy's small breasts were tucked neatly away in her unlined bralette, and her barely-there thong panties showed she was freshly shaven. Emily stopped to take in the sight in front of her.

I wasn't sure I'd be this aroused with anyone else, she thought as flashes of her and Anika's time together started to flood her mind. Emily closed her eyes and sat up.

Pulling at the hem of her sweater, Izzy helped Emily take if off to reveal her blue and black bra. Emily's large breasts threatened to spill over, and Izzy looked on appreciatively as Emily slipped out of her leggings and revealed matching panties.

Emily pulled the covers down on her bed and crawled in, leaving room for Izzy. They pulled the blankets up as their mouths met again. Emily found Izzy's nipple under the thin bra. Izzy let out a surprised groan as her nipple erected at the pressure between Emily's finger and thumb.

Izzy laughed at her reaction and said, "It's been a while since I've been with anyone."

"I understand that," Emily replied as she kissed Izzy deeply and allowed her hands to travel over her bum and caress closer to Izzy's warmth.

Izzy rolled on top of Emily. She kissed down her jaw and neck and moved lower to kiss her chest. Reaching behind Emily, Izzy undid her bra and pulled it forward. She tossed it aside and kissed all around her breast, finally arriving at her nipple.

Emily cried out as Izzy brought it into her mouth and gently sucked. Slipping her tongue around and around, Emily found herself pressing herself against Izzy's leg as her wetness grew. She ran her hands through Izzy's short hair and over the soft skin of her shoulders.

Izzy kissed across to the other breast and repeated her tongue movements. Then, flicking both nipples gently, Izzy slowly kissed down Emily's soft belly and bit her hip gently as she picked up the edge of her underwear in her mouth. Emily made eye contact with Izzy and let out a groan of need.

Izzy slid Emily's panties off slowly, bringing goosebumps to the other's skin as Izzy's fingers and lips grazed the inside of her foot and up her calf and thigh. Slowly, Izzy nibbled her way to Emily's wetness. Emily cried out in anticipation then rolled her head back as Izzy finally brought her lips to her clit and flicked it with her tongue.

"Izzy …" Emily called out as she reached for her head to bring Izzy's mouth deeper.

Izzy flicked faster and Emily cried out. Rolling her hips and reaching her hands behind her head to hold on to the pillow. Crying out again, Emily lurched forward and met Izzy's eyes as she allowed herself release.

As Emily's orgasm subsided, she pulled Izzy back on top of her. Her perfume filled Emily's senses and they lay quietly. She ran her fingertips over Izzy's back and ass, then up her side. It sent a wave of goosebumps over Izzy's body that made her shiver and giggle.

Their mouths met again in slow kisses. Emily could taste herself on Izzy and it turned her on. Kissing down her neck, Emily reached behind Izzy to free her breasts. Slipping the straps from her arms, Emily ran her hands over them and played with her nipples, Emily watched Izzy's face flush and her mouth open slightly at the gentle pinch of Emily's fingers.

Emily finally brought her mouth to Izzy's nipple and gently sucked and played with it. She pushed away comparisons of Anika's and Izzy's bodies from her mind and continued to enjoy the small erect tip she ran over and between her lips.

Emily slid down the bed to take all of Izzy in. Her pale skin was flushed, nipples erect. Izzy's underwear was still on, and Emily slowly slid them down to reveal a strip of perfectly shaven pubic hair and a piercing.

Emily felt herself moisten again and quickly threw Izzy's underwear on the floor as she spread the other's legs to reveal her wetness.

Emily played at the opening of Izzy's folds, spreading her juices over her pierced clit. She brought her mouth to Izzy and, with the long, slow strokes of her tongue, she lapped up Izzy's wetness.

She abruptly stopped when Izzy cried out.

"Sorry ... Are you okay? I've never ..." Emily looked down at the Izzy's piercing and back at her face.

"All good. It's very sensitive but I'm enjoying what you're doing," she panted.

"Good." Emily smiled and brought her mouth back to Izzy's folds.

Izzy cried out again in short high-pitched tones as she neared her climax. Cupping her breast, Emily watched Izzy play with her own nipple, twisting and pulling it away from her, getting harder the closer she got to coming.

Izzy let out a loud cry and wriggled beneath Emily, pushing her hips into Emily's mouth. Emily pushed her tongue into Izzy and felt the warmth spread over her face as the orgasm flooded her body.

Emily pulled the covers up over them both as she lay down in Izzy's chest. Listening to her heart slow and breathing ease, Emily sighed and closed her eyes. *This feels nice.*

Izzy was the first to stir, "Emily?" she asked quietly.

"Uh-huh," Emily mumbled in reply, eyes still closed, her arm around Izzy's slight waist. Izzy stroked her hair and pushed it from Emily's face.

Emily looked up to meet Izzy's eyes. Izzy smiled. "We should probably get back to Andrea's, I guess."

"Yes."

"I enjoyed tonight." Emily kissed Izzy's lips softly, running her tongue over them, and got out of bed.

"So did I. Are you okay with all of this?" Izzy gestured to the bed as she put her panties and bra back on.

"Yes …" Emily paused, suddenly feeling the weight of what they had just done, "It's … well, you're the first person I've been with since Conrad and Anika. It feels like finality."

Izzy embraced Emily. "We didn't have to do anything if you felt uncomfortable. If you didn't want to."

"I did want to. I want to again," Emily laughed, sniffling away tears.

Izzy laughed and kissed Emily's lips tenderly. They made comfortable small talk about dinner while they finished dressing. Emily called a cab while Izzy used the washroom.

They left the apartment hand-in-hand.

CHAPTER 24

Emily awoke in her bed alone. She could hear her girls playing quietly with each other. She rolled over and looked at the time: 7:00.

First day of summer break, she thought to herself with a smile. Picking up her phone, she saw she had several missed text messages from Anika. Sitting up with concern, Emily began reading through them, each getting shorter.

11:45pm: Emily … I think we need to talk. I guess you didn't know we were in town on Saturday. I saw you. We saw you. You were having dinner with a woman. You were holding hands with her. Seems like you were more than friends. I thought you promised to tell me when you decided to move on.

1:09am: I don't really care what you do with your life. You should have just been honest with me.

1:13am: I hope you're not ignoring me … I deserve more than that.

1:22am: I hope you're happy with whoever that was.

1:44am: GOOD NIGHT

Emily shook her head and sat up. She went in search of the girls and gave them both hugs then prepared oatmeal for them as she made coffee. While it brewed, Emily dialed Anika's number. Her call went to voicemail, and Emily hung up before the message finished.

"Damn," she said out loud.

Looking down at the phone's black screen. Emily went out onto the apartment's small deck with the fresh coffee and turned to watch the traffic below. The late June day was sunny, and they were looking forward to fireworks in a few days for the Canada Day celebration. She sipped her coffee as she listened to her daughters' happy sounds as they ate breakfast and discussed their summer plans.

Emily tried Anika again and was about to hang up when she answered.

"Hi," Anika answered curtly.

"Hi," Emily replied. Emily played with her mug and stared over the treetops. "Do you want to talk?"

"I'm not sure there's much to say, Emily." More silence. "You promised you'd tell me if there were someone else."

"I didn't lie to you."

"Omission is the same as lying."

"I didn't omit. I'm allowed to have friends. I don't have to run them all by you just because they are women. I had no idea that anything was going to develop between me and Izzy. I wasn't looking for anything."

"Yeah," Anika scoffed, with a nasally laugh. "You weren't looking for something with Matisse and I either, right?"

"I'm not sure what that's supposed to mean."

"Seems like you always take the easy way out. You just let people get hurt. You're too much of a coward to take the responsibility on yourself."

"I'm the coward?" Emily voice got louder, and she felt tears build as her anger grew, "I'm not the one who promised they'd leave their husband I ever left mine. I'm not the one who showed up time and time again to get fulfillment of the sex they couldn't get any where else. I'm not the one who let you down by promising to be there for you during one of the most stressful and heartbreaking times in your life, then take the side of the person who broke you. I've done nothing but be supportive and patient and understanding with you. You've hardly been any of those things.

"I can't do this anymore, Anika," Emily kept her voice calm and wiped the last of the tears from her face. She spoke matter-of-factly, emotion devoid from her speech, "I'm tired of feeling like I'm not important and being worried that at some point you're just going to cut me off without warning."

"You've made this a bigger deal than it needed to be."

"You've done nothing but support Conrad and tear me down since I left him. You've never really been on my side."

"I've been on your side plenty. You're the one who lied to me and decided to keep things from me."

Emily got up and paced on the small deck. "I'm not going to argue about whether or not I hid something from you. You're going to believe whatever you feel like. I'm sorry I hurt you. But we both know *we* weren't going anywhere." Emily paused. "Did you know Matisse and I had lunch back in February?"

"No ..." Anika said quietly.

"He spotted me in Costco and asked if we could have lunch."

"So, what? He's allowed to have lunch with people. He knows you."

"True, but he spent the hour explaining how his feelings for me haven't changed, and that he still wishes we could be together. Without you."

"Why are you telling me this now? Trying to clear your conscious of the things you've hidden from me?"

Emily heard faint sniffling on the other end. "That's not what I'm doing. I told him I wasn't interested at all and never had the same sort of feelings for him as he had for me. I told him to be a better husband to you. That you sacrificed a lot to make things work with him. I didn't want to hurt you. I love you, Anika. I wanted to wait for you, but I can't wait forever."

"I know, Emily."

The phone beeped. She looked down to see the call had ended. She balled up her fists and breathed deeply. Letting her breath out, she let her shoulders go loose. Bringing her empty coffee cup to the kitchen for a refill, she made plans with her daughters for the day and the week ahead.

CHAPTER 25

Emily soaked in the bath. The water was hot enough to almost feel cold on her skin. It made her body fill with goosebumps as she slid into it.

She didn't mind the pleasurable pain. It reminded her that she was still alive. She looked at her arms under the water.

She knew she made the right decision by leaving Conrad. He'd ignored her and treated her with such disdain that she began to believe there was something wrong with herself. He gaslighted her into feeling bad about any type of selfcare, and it became almost impossible for her to tell the difference between reality and fiction.

Emily had enough. She refused to live like that any longer, and she refused to allow her daughters to be raised like that. They needed a strong mother and role model. She finally made progress to move on. Her budding relationship with Izzy had taken her mind off Conrad and Anika.

Tonight, she didn't feel very strong. She had just gotten off the phone with her sister. Their brother had died.

There weren't many details yet, but everyone was shocked. Emily cried silently in her bath and felt empty. There was a piece missing now. One she hadn't even realized was there. She and her brother didn't grow up together. In fact, she really didn't know him very well at all.

However, since her and Conrad had separated, Nathan started calling more to restore his relationship with Emily. It was a complicated one with years of distance and a father who tried to manipulate every situation between the siblings.

Emily looked again at the scars and then at a razor sitting on the edge of the tub. She picked it up, placed it on her upper forearm and used just enough pressure to draw a thin line of blood. It didn't hurt, not yet. She knew it took more than that to make it hurt.

She removed the blade from her arm and stared at the small cut. She screwed up her face and threw the razor across the bathroom. Emily slid under the water and screamed, watching the bubbles escape her and pop on the surface. She remembered back to the conversation she'd had with Anika.

"You shouldn't have called the police," Anika told Emily after Conrad had called her from the police station. "He's just struggling. He just needs some guidance right now. You left him alone and without you or the kids, without warning."

"I did warn him," Emily had explained desperately, hoping to convince Anika to be on her side, "I told him for years that I wasn't happy. I gave him the choice for months to support my career and want to be with me. I gave him chances –"

"I guess," Anika said, "but men are dumb. You need to be blunt with them. He missed you and the kids."

Emily didn't agree. She didn't see Conrad as lonely and lost. He tried to manipulate anyone he could into being on his side. Into believing his story. Emily knew she had to stand her ground, but it hurt her to no end that Anika didn't believe her or, rather, didn't want to support her like she'd said she would.

She naively believed that her and Anika plans for a life together would mean fellowship and support between them. Anika was only committed to them being together when it meant Emily would stay with Conrad and their lives wouldn't change all that much:

Emily would be with Conrad; Anika would be with Matisse. Emily and Anika would be together when they could and be able to express their raw emotion and sexual tension with each other. Yet, their lives wouldn't really change much.

Emily didn't want to live in a fantasy world where she hid the true self and emotions from herself and the rest of the world. She didn't want Claire and Julia growing up thinking it was best to be what someone else wanted you to believe. She didn't want them growing up with a mother whose sobs could be heard in the bathroom late at night.

Emily stepped out of the bath and looked back down at her phone again. She reluctantly left the screen where Anika's name was and instead texted Izzy:

I know this is last minute, but I just got some terrible news. I hope you're free tonight. I could really use a friend.

Emily stared at the message for a few moments, then sent it out. She knew she was putting herself out there, but she also knew what she needed right now. She needed to be loved. She needed to be cared for and caressed.

Emily had only really started to get to know Izzy over the past month, but she felt a deep connection with her. She desperately hoped it was more than just a passing crush for either of them, but Emily knew she needed to be a bit guarded and reserved.

There were a lot of things so very different about the two of them. Not just their personalities, but their lifestyles. Maybe it would work, maybe it wouldn't. But right now, Emily knew what she needed, and she was tired of putting her needs aside.

I will be there soon. I hope you are okay. xo

Emily's eyes filled with tears as she read Izzy's text. She doubted whether she would come, but better than Izzy just coming, she hadn't questioned Emily at all. She hadn't questioned why she needed her, or what happened. Izzy had decided she would be there.

Twenty minutes later, Emily let Izzy into her apartment. She stood there silently, shoulders slumped, hair still a mess from her bath, arms at her sides, expressionless. "My brother died this morning."

Izzy stared at Emily for a moment then quickly strode the distance between them and embraced her. "I am so sorry, Emily. I am so sorry."

Emily fell limply into Izzy, arms still at her side. She sobbed so hard her legs felt weak and wanted to buckle. She sobbed so hard her stomach hurt and her eyes had no tears left.

Izzy rubbed her back and held her up. They stood at the entryway for a long time before Emily finally broke away. Her blotched face tear-stained and pained.

"I'll make us some tea," Izzy escorted Emily to a stool at the bar. She put the water on, then went to the liquor cabinet. Taking out two shot glasses, she took a bottle of Jack from her purse and poured them generous shots. "To Nathan."

"To Nathan," Emily repeated.

They clinked and downed the burning liquid. Izzy refilled them as they waited for the kettle to boil. The women looked at each other. Only this moment mattered – right now. There was nothing else on either of their minds as they stared at each other.

"Thank you," Emily whispered.

We are proud to present an excerpt of the
next book from Vanessa M. Thibeault:
Devil in Their Veins

"Mom! Mom! Watch me, Mom!" Three-year-old Greyson shouted to Sheri as he climbed to the top of the monkey bars.

She didn't hear her son at first because she was speaking to Greyson's father, Ken. From the boy's perspective, the conversation seemed serious as his mother flung her arms up and pointed in Greyson's direction. Eyebrows close together frantically moving lips gave way to the anger she was spilling.

Bleach blond hair with inch long roots gave her social status away, as did the cigarette hanging from her hand as she talked. Her worn khaki shorts and tube top, which didn't hide anything, were one fad behind, and they didn't fit quite the way they were supposed to. Meanwhile Ken's jeans and white t-shirt hugged his large, trim body.

"Mom!" Greyson called again, climbing higher, too high for his still developing coordination. Sheri continued to ignore him.

"You promised me last month that you'd pay! You can't keep skipping out. He needs you. I need your support. I can't get him into day care, and my mom'll only watch him two days a week." Sherri's anger gave way to desperation.

"You just want the money for drugs. I ain't paying for your habit. Besides, I don't even know he's mine," Ken stood calm and glared at Sheri. He took a pack of smokes from one front pocket of his jeans and a lighter from the other. Lighting a cigarette, he breathed in deeply and blew the smoke in her face.

"You're fucking kiddin' right? Not yours? He's a fucking spitting image," she spat at Ken and pointed in his face. "And unlike you, I wasn't fucking around."

"Yeah," Ken laughed, "Kinda hard to deny that one, I guess. But it's been almost three years, Sher. You need to figure this out. I'm not paying, considerin' you're the one who kicked me out. I have one on the way anyways. I just came here to see the boy. Tell you I'm leaving town soon."

"Like hell you are! Who's the whore mother of this child, Ken? Oh, let me guess, June?" Sheri straightened up, her five-foot-one frame stretching to its tallest, and spit at Ken's feet as the name came out of her mouth. "That's the same whore you were sleeping with right after Grey was born, ain't it?"

"That's none of your fucking business, bitch," Ken cussed at her easily, the word sliding off his tongue. Words he used far too often to describe the women in his life.

"Mom!" Greyson called again, louder this time, finally gaining his mother's attention.

"Get down from there!" she yelled at him, rushing toward the playground. "Get down! Now!"

Greyson obeyed, wanting to please his mother, yet feeling disappointed that she hadn't noticed his efforts. He always wanted her approval. He wanted to listen, but he needed her attention as well. It was attention he always had to share with other men in his life.

"Go play on the swings," she suggested, pushing him toward the less dangerous playground equipment.

"Okay, mom." Greyson recognized the man his mom argued with but couldn't place him right now. He felt unsure about him and he was uncomfortable watching them argue. Even at his age, Greyson felt the need to protect his mother.

Ken watched Greyson run to the swings and struggle to get his chubby toddler body onto the seat. Finally accomplishing his task, Greyson started to rock back and forth.

"Does the boy even know, Sher?" Ken inquired, both annoyed and curious.

"I've tried to keep him as innocent as possible. You haven't exactly been around, Ken."

"A boy's gotta know who his father is. You don't get to take that away from him."

"You haven't been around. What's I'm supposed to tell him?"

206

"Don't worry, I'll do it, Sher." He brushed her off, annoyed. He took a step toward the swings, taking a long drag on his cigarette, blowing out and puffing again. Sheri stepped in front of him, placing her hands on his chest.

"Don't you even think about tellin' him, Ken!"

"Not up to you anymore," he replied.

"No," she said, less confidently, but still standing her ground. Grey may have been Ken's blood, but she had raised him. Grey was her son and he deserved better than the deadbeat she'd allowed to father him.

However, something nagged at her. She was tired of doing it alone, and she wasn't convinced that keeping Ken out of Grey's life was the best choice. A boy needed his father.

"Get your fucking hands off me," Ken pushed Sherri roughly aside and she stumbled, tripping over the border that lined the playground. She fell to her knees, blond hair covering her face.

"Ken!" she yelled to his back. With no response she muttered, "Fucking bastard."

"Hey, Grey," Ken started casually as he made his way toward the swing. "What's up?"

Greyson eyed this man carefully. There was an essence of familiarity which surrounded him. His face looked familiar as did his body language. Ken went around behind Greyson and started pushing him.

"You hurt my mom," Grey replied simply, untrusting.

"Nah, she just tripped," Ken answered passively. "You like hockey, buddy."

"Yeah," Greyson was still unsure of this man. His gut told him not to trust him, but his toddler mind wanted to think of happier things. Things that made him feel good. Ken stopped the swing and came around to look Greyson in the eye.

"Me too," Ken replied, "I used to play. Was real good, too."

"Really?" Greyson's eyes lit up.

"Sure did," Ken reached into his back pocket and pulled out his wallet. Opening it, he took out a minor league hockey card of himself from six years ago.

"Cool!" Greyson exclaimed, taking the card excitedly from Ken.

"You can keep that."

"Thanks, mister," Greyson replied happily, the unease he felt almost completely gone with the thought of his very own hockey card of a real person he'd met.

"There something else, too," Ken said. "Your mom's never told you much about your dad, has she?"

"No." Greyson had asked his mom where his dad was when friends in his apartment complex brought theirs outside to play catch or ball hockey in the street.

"Well, that there in your hand is a picture of your dad."

Greyson stared hard at the card for a moment then looked from it to the man kneeling in front of him. A man that looked too familiar to have been seen at the grocery store. Someone who stirred too much emotion in his mother to not be of importance.

"That's enough, Ken," Sheri found her voice and her courage and stood between him and Greyson. He hugged his mother's leg and peeked out from the side. She held a protective hand on his head. "You've done enough. Just stop, before you confuse the boy."

"There's nothing to confuse him about, Sher. Just letting him know who his father is. Just want him to remember this face." The warm smile Ken tried to produce seemed fake. It didn't reach his eyes.

Those eyes were what scared Greyson. When he looked into them, he saw nothing but bad. Bad intentions, bad ideas, bad moods, and bad decisions.

"Mom?" Greyson questioned, looking up at her with his father's big blue eyes. "That's my dad?"

Sheri looked down at her son, trapped. She couldn't lie to him with Ken standing right there. One the other hand, she dreaded the thought of admitting her huge mistake. She should have never let this man into her life. She shouldn't have let him have the part of her which would always be connected her son. She prayed Greyson wouldn't get the same temperament as his father.

"Umm …." She started.

"I sure am, pal." Ken kneeled back down and peeked around Sheri's leg, staring into Greyson's eyes.

"Oh." Was all Greyson could manage. He felt scared and couldn't place the other feeling as he examined Ken's reflected blue eyes. One that carried deep secrets and damage.

"It's time you went, Ken." Sheri spoke again, trying to assert herself for Greyson. She hated this man for giving her this child. Sometimes she thought she should have listened to Ken and gotten rid of her son before he was even big enough to be considered a human being. But right now, her bond and instinct to protect Greyson made her step between the life she never wanted and the one she tried to develop. One where she stood up for what she thought was the right thing.

ABOUT THE AUTHOR

Vanessa lives in British Columbia in the sunny valley of Okanagan. She spends her time reading, gardening, cooking, and raising her daughters. She spends her evenings with close friends enjoying great wine and company.

Publications include: Transcendent Publishing's *The Peacemakers: Restoring Love in the world through Stories of Compassion and Wisdom* (Transcendent Publishing, 2016), *All of Me, All of You* (Transcendent Publishing, 2017), and two short stories in Electric Press's online literary magazine *Float* and *Restitution*.

"A life that is not dull is one not without inspiration. I hope to inspire those to find strength within themselves, as that's the only place true strength comes from. The only limit is your own self-doubt." -VMT

Connect with me at:
- Website: www.vanessamthibeault.ca
- Amazon Author Page: www.amazon.com/Vanessa-Thibeualt/B01MZILXQQ
- Twitter: @vmthibeaultCA
- Facebook: vanessamthibeault
- Goodreads at Vanessa M. Thibeault

Made in the USA
Monee, IL
08 October 2021

79181565R00125